DEDICATION

In Loving Memory of

Rozelle Vogelman

Illegitimi Non Carborundum

BRILLIANT CHARMING BASTARD

GETTING RICH IS THE BEST REVENGE

STELLA FOSSE

ISBN: 978-1-950227-06-8

Cover art by dianarosinus.com

Published by:

Baubo Books

125 S Estes Drive #4311,

Chapel Hill, NC 27514, USA

www.stellafosse.com

I'D LOVE TO KNOW YOU BETTER!

I write a regular blog and newsletter. A blog comes out — either from me or from a guest blogger[1] — on the 10th and 20th of the month. That's always related to being a woman past mid-life or the craft of writing [you can find my manifesto at https://stellafosse.com/stella-fosse-author-erotic-writer/#Manifesto], and a Newsletter once a month at the end of the month.

You can sign up for my Newsletter & Blog on my website: www.stellafosse.com

---

1. Want to write a guest blog? I welcome drafts or suggestions for promoting YOUR writing or thoughts there. You should be 'on topic' for my blog - see my manifesto for the topics that I cover on my blog and website. The requirements for submission are here: stellafosse.com/stella-fosse-author-erotic-writer/#Submissions

CONTENTS

[1]

THE OPTICAL LIMITS OF ROSE-COLORED GLASSES

I nstead of bringing a bouquet as when they first dated, Brendan carried a bag with his CPAP machine when he knocked on Rose's door.

His hostess answered. "Come in! I was just making enchiladas."

"Good. I won't disturb you." He made himself at home at the living room computer, where his eyes never left the screen.

Rose stood at the stove assembling dinner, glancing at her guest through the door of her kitchen. With his round shape and white beard, he looked more like Santa Claus than a movie star. Still, there was something about him. He joked about his appearance but was proud of his vision. Brendan flew Navy jets in the Vietnam War, or so he said. To hear him talk, this man who lived in a rundown house with a beat-up car had been a physician and inventor. Who knew how much was true? But his vision remained perfect, and she found the gaze from his bright blue eyes compelling.

Rose remembered evenings months earlier, when she hovered near him as he cooked in his aisle kitchen. She made conversation and fetched ingredients, excited because she knew they would make love after dinner. This was a different evening.

It had been a week since Rose last saw Brendan, but they had emailed. She worried they were not seeing each other as often as they had. He wrote back, sent her a love poem by Pablo Neruda, told her she should love him and trust him more. They should talk, he said, from a loving place. He invited her to dinner.

"No," she said. "Let me cook for you this time." So he was here, but so far they were not talking.

"This is good," he offered at dinner, and scarfed down two helpings of green enchiladas with Spanish rice. Afterwards he grabbed the remote and turned on the television. She left the dishes in the sink and joined him on the couch, still hoping to talk. But Brendan focussed on the show. "Time to turn in," he said when it ended.

They climbed into bed, both of them naked. He turned away and reached for a journal from his overnight bag.

It was her last chance to start a conversation. "So, you haven't said what you've been up to lately."

"Mmm?" He kept reading.

"I haven't seen you in a while."

He put down his journal abruptly. "There's no need for us to be joined at the hip. You and I will just keep getting closer. I know you better than your family does."

Rose ran her fingers down his cushioned back. "You certainly know me differently than they know me. And speaking of that..."

He glanced over his shoulder at her. "I am reading an important document. And when I finish, I will go to sleep—as should you. Really, Rose, don't you have a lecture in the morning? You're a biologist. You know that sex is less important as we age." With an abrupt flourish, he put down the journal and turned on his CPAP with its breathy faux astronaut sounds. Once the mask was on his face, Brendan could not talk and acted like he could not hear. He turned out the light.

She knew from experience that once the machine was on, he wanted her to lie there quietly. But after two hours sleepless by his side while he snuffled into his CPAP, her bare skin tingling with desire and his soft with sleep, she had to get out of bed. She put on her nightgown, opened the bedroom door and walked into the kitchen, closing the door quietly behind her.

The Art Deco clock built into the old stove ticked midnight as Rose washed the dinner dishes, her grey-dyed-brown hair tucked behind her ears. She hummed a Linda Ronstadt tune and pushed up her glasses with the back of one wet hand. Never mind the noise. Brendan hated waking in the night not knowing where she was. But this time if he woke, he could trace her by the sounds of water running and dishes colliding in the sink.

She heard Brendan curse through the wall. Rose dried her hands and opened the bedroom door. He had turned the light back on. There he was, Santa in a bathrobe, wrapping his CPAP and packing to go.

She sat on the edge of her bed. "I don't want you to leave."

"I know," he said. "And there's nothing for me at home. But you need to learn self-control. You have responsibilities in the morning. And by our age, sex should mean little more than gender." Rose thought of objecting that she wasn't his age, he had seven years on her, but that seemed petty. Then Brendan switched off the bedroom light, walked through the living room and out the front door.

Rose followed him and cracked open the door. The taillights of his old Mercedes receded and were gone. Good riddance. All was quiet on her little street. The bungalows were lined up under the streetlight with their grey stucco walls and wood frame windows. Victorian boxwood trees scented the night. She closed the door firmly and threw the security bolt.

As she headed back to bed, Rose glanced with satisfaction at the living room of her Berkeley cottage, decorated just to her liking in Early Cretaceous. There were model dinosaurs on the coffee table and ferns in copper pots on the hardwood floor.

Either Brendan would be back someday or he would not. And either she would take him back or she would not. Time would tell. At least now she could sleep.

First, though, to finish the dishes. And if, in the process, one slipped from her hands and crashed to the floor, perhaps it was the plate on which Brendan ate his last meal in Rose's cozy bungalow.

R ose slept, but at four in the morning she awoke for no apparent reason. Around her the house was quiet and dark. She had no pets to make noise, only the fossils, silent on the shelf. She put on her robe and wandered the rooms, checking each window in the little house. First the windows in her bedroom, and then she walked through the Jack-and-Jill bathroom to the room that had been her daughter Linda's, where granddaughter Ella now slept when she stayed over. All good. Then Rose checked the kitchen and living room windows. Everything was fine.

Her computer was still on. When she went to shut it down, she saw that Brendan had left his email open. Rose sat in her desk chair and looked at the screen. *I should shut it down,* she thought. *Without looking. This isn't right.*

Rose did not shut down Brendan's email, but neither did she touch a thing. She just stared at the titles in his inbox about engineering and medicine and space launches. On the left side of the screen was a folder marked "Personal." A subfolder listed her name: *Rose Bingham.* There were two other names. Who were these women? Brendan frequently discoursed on past relationships and the women who had failed him, but these names were unfamiliar. She clicked a subfolder: *Maxine Vargas.* She opened an email called *"The Two of You."* It was dated just a week ago, and the title was familiar.

"My Darling Maxine...
Yes, I agree we should talk, but only if we can interact productively.
If you can set aside your doubts, your negativity, your mistrust, then
we can have a positive conversation.
If you cannot do that, then perhaps I am not the one for you."

Dear God, thought Rose, *I remember this; next he's going to invite just her higher self to dinner.*

"And so, I would like you to come to me, the real you, the loving you.
I will prepare delights a deux, for only us to share.
Leave her at home, that doubting Maxine. I can see her another time."

And now comes the fricking Neruda poem, thought Rose.

"I am reminded of a love song by the great poet Pablo Neruda..."

"Oh shit," Rose said aloud. And then she opened the other subfolder, the one marked Joyce Farrell, where she found the same email:

"My Darling Joyce, Yes, I agree we should talk, but only if we can interact productively..."

"Self-plagiarism: The lowest form of flattery," Rose said to the empty house. "Well, Brendan. So much for your flipping self-control. Also known as Joyce and Maxine."

Carefully, without disturbing his email account, she opened her own account and found an email Brendan had sent to her, also called "The Two of You."

"My Darling Rose..." it began, *"Yes, I agree we should talk..."*

Rose pressed Forward, added email addresses for Joyce and Maxine and a brief introduction.

"Greetings to the two of you," she wrote, "This email I received from Brendan Burns may sound familiar. Best regards, Rose Bingham."

He's right: It really is a shame that I lack self-control, Rose mused, as the cursor hovered over Send.

So tempting. But was it a good idea? Would it be kind or cruel to contact these women?

The sun was up. She must get ready for her morning lecture at the University. That would give her time to cool off.

Or not.

[2]

THE INVITATION

I sis Hamilton caught sight of Dr. Bingham as she crossed the big grass quad down the hill from Life Sciences. Isis was on the Track and Field team and had no trouble catching up. Once she was next to her teacher, Isis slowed down to match the older woman's stride. Dr. Bingham looked thoughtful, even preoccupied. How grand to be so immersed in research that a walk across campus was a chance to ponder the mysteries of life.

"Dr. Bingham? May I walk with you? If I'm not interrupting."

"No, that's fine, Isis. I'm glad to see you." Rose looked up at the tall African American woman in the track suit. Isis was an engineering major who asked great questions at Rose's lectures.

"I was thinking over what you said about codons."

"Oh, really?"

"Yes. And how the chart shows there are different DNA codes for the same amino acid."

"That's right. As many as four, for some of them."

"It's funny how our brains work. When you said that it reminded me that there are lots of fish in the sea. Men, I mean. Not just one that would work." Isis laughed. "Silly, I know. It's just because I'm twenty that I worry about these things. By your age I'm sure you have all this personal stuff figured out."

"Oh, you'd be surprised, Isis—"

"No, I saw you, walking across the quad, your mind on your research. I kind of envy you, being able to devote your brain power to your field. I can't wait to be past all this drama. I thought it was just for teenagers, but I'm not a teen anymore."

"Isis."

"Yeah?"

"Let's say you were dating a guy and it turned out he was seeing two other women without telling you. If one of them figured it out, would you want her to say? Or would you want her to stay out of your business?"

Isis stopped walking. "So, you weren't thinking about biology just now."

Rose stopped too and laughed. "I suppose this is biology. Everything we do is biology."

"That's fair." Isis frowned. "OK, here's what I think. At first, I'd be mad at her. I guess that's just human."

"Right. They call that impulse 'shoot the messenger.'"

"OK. But then I'd be glad she told me so I could kick his sorry ass. And then I'd be mad at myself for not figuring it out on my own."

"Ah. So, if you were the woman who figured it out, would you tell the others?"

"Yeah. Women have to stick together."

"Yes, I can see that."

Isis looked at Dr. Bingham. "Sounds like you've got people to call after class, Dr. B."

"Maybe I do. And maybe you should be the one to teach today. You've certainly taught me something."

"Glad I could help. But don't go getting on the phone or whatever yet. I need you to lecture about those twisty shapes proteins make when they're built."

"Protein conformation."

"Yeah, how does that work? Can you talk about that?"

"Sure, Isis. It's a deal."

People passed them now, moving faster. Up on the Campanile, the clock edged toward the hour.

Isis started walking. "Come on. We need to get to class. And you can't run as fast as I can."

* * *

The San Francisco Bay laps at the western edge of Berkeley, where artists build driftwood statues in the sand. From the shoreline east to the campus of the University of California is the neighborhood called the Flats, a bastion of liberal politics once known for inexpensive housing. In the center of town is the Berkeley campus, known simply as Cal because it was the first campus of the University of California. With its mix of Spanish and modern architecture, Cal is a verdant oasis dominated by the Campanile, a soaring clock tower with daily carillon concerts. East of campus the Berkeley Hills provide splendid bay views and elegant homes for well-heeled hipsters.

Rose was not well-heeled; no hills mansion for her. As a young professor in the 1980s, a newly divorced Rose had bought her little place in the Flats. Not for the first time, Rose was glad her house was close enough to walk home for lunch. Not that she wanted to eat; her stomach was in knots. But it was great to be in her own refuge. There had been a time near the end of the pandemic when Rose never wanted to see her house again. She had felt trapped, claustrophobic, in her tidy little space. But a year later she could appreciate her restful environment. She regretted letting Brendan into her home last night, but if she hadn't, how would she have discovered his charade?

Once home, she logged onto her computer and found her draft email.

Were these two women as invested in Brendan as she? Was it any of her business whether they knew the truth? Was Rose being a terrible busybody? Turning into a little old lady who watches her neighbors through lace curtains? Would it be a mistake to send that email?

Yes, it would be a mistake. Absolutely. The hell with it. She clicked send.

Rose stared at the screen; she did not know why. Did she think it would explode? Would lightning strike? Really, she should try to eat something and then head for the lab. She should open a can of soup. She had experiments to check and office hours to attend.

And then, even though it was the middle of a workday, two emails popped up. Rose opened each in turn.

From Joyce Farrell: "Yes, this email sounds familiar. Who are you? How did you get my contact info? And how do you know Brendan?"

And from Maxine Vargas only this: "I would like to know more."

With an odd thrill, a sense that nothing would ever be the same, Rose typed a new email inviting Joyce and Maxine to meet her, tonight, right after work.

"Meet me at The Lab, that bar on Powell Street. The drinks are on me."

[3]
MEETING AT "THE LAB"

The Lab was Rose's favorite bar, a woman-owned tavern at the center of the East Bay biotech scene. It was an appealing open space on the first floor of a new apartment building in Emeryville, a manufacturing town turned techno hub. As she walked in, Rose greeted the bartender, a sturdy short-haired woman who was one of the owners. Drinks were served in glassware shaped like beakers, periodic tables were decoupaged on bar tables, and pictures of women scientists with pithy quotations were framed on the walls. Rose had arranged to meet Maxine and Joyce at a corner table, beneath a quote from Marie Curie: "Be less curious about people and more about ideas." Seemed like good advice, but Rose was terribly curious about the women sitting across from her.

Dr. Joyce Farrell turned out to be a chemist from Sirona Pharmaceuticals, right there in Emeryville. She was in her mid-sixties, a pale woman with auburn hair turning gray. Joyce had the solid look of a woman who lifted weights for fun. Maxine Vargas was about the same age, a well-tailored African

American lawyer who had succeeded in the white male world of intellectual property. They were impressive women. Whatever else you could say about Brendan, he had excellent taste.

Rose told them about the night she discovered their emails. Then the three of them sat silent for a moment. Joyce roused herself to speak. "So, he refuses to have sex with you, and then tells you that you should have more self-control. Then he walks out and leaves our emails open on your computer."

"That's right."

"Clearly he had no problem sending each of us the same email." Joyce sounded frustrated.

"Clearly not," said Rose.

"And you decided to show us," said Joyce.

"Uh-huh." Rose wondered who annoyed Joyce more: Brendan or her?

"And you thought you were doing us a favor."

"No. Not really." Rose was almost enjoying herself. "I was just pissed off."

"Well, thanks a lot—"

At this, Maxine stepped in. "Let's back it up a minute. I want to know how this started. Rose, how did you meet this guy?"

"The attorney begins the cross examination." Joyce had plenty of anger to go around.

"Swing and a miss, Joyce. I write patents for a living. I don't go to court. Rose, how did you find Brendan? Did you meet him online?"

"Yes," said Rose, thinking back, "It was my daughter's idea. About a year ago, at the end of the pandemic. She and my granddaughter were tired of me moping around their house. And my daughter had a great plan for how to occupy my time. Or so she thought."

* * *

Linda Bingham Jones lived in a comfortable ranch house in Walnut Creek, on the East side of the Berkeley hills, with her husband Rick and their daughter Ella. That Saturday afternoon was bright and sunny. Walnut Creek was almost always sunny, unlike Rose's lovely foggy Berkeley.

Linda and Rose sat side by side in the living room, staring at a computer screen. Across the room Ella sprawled on the couch wearing ear buds and glued to her cell phone, in a world of her own. Family gatherings looked like this now, Rose thought. During the pandemic she imagined they would take picnics and hike together when it was over, but here they were, stuck to their screens. On the other hand, was it any better when she was Ella's age, when the family watched Lawrence Welk together?

Linda was a brunette as Rose had been (and still was, with chemical enhancement). They sat with heads together. Linda was on a mission.

"See, Mom? Just answer some questions, and the system offers you people you might like—people with things in common."

"Yes, I see."

Linda pulled up a prospect. "Like this one. He looks interesting." She read aloud from the screen.

"'Among my prior (abundant) amorous friends and my (alas, too few) beloveds, it is invariably the case that our sexiest organs are betwixt our ears.'"

"Oh, for heaven's sake, Linda!" Rose glanced at Ella, who was blessedly oblivious in cellphone land.

Linda kept reading. "'And no matter how visually enticing a woman may be, my Eros will evaporate without an adventuresome mind, a gleeful enjoyment of life, and a keen and ironic humor.' My goodness, he's a poet! 'My Eros will evaporate.' He even alliterates!"

Rose could feel her face turn red. "That's enough, Linda. Whatever happened to meeting people in person? At a bookstore, or at church? Good grief, the pandemic is over."

"So, have you met anyone in person? No, right? Think about online dating, Mom. You should have some happiness."

"I am happy. I enjoy teaching. And I love taking care of our Ella."

"Ella is growing up. Just look at her: she pays way more attention to her friends than she does to you or me. How about some happiness just for you?"

"I will think about it, Linda. Thank you for showing me this."

"Sure, Mom. You have a profile now. You can access it any time. You can write to this guy if you want."

That evening at home, Rose opened the website and looked at the profile of the fellow Linda had found. Was he fascinating, or just full of hot air? And what would happen if she messaged him? Realizing, of course, that "message" was not really a verb, but one of those constructed monstrosities that used to be restricted to corporations and advertisements. And if she wrote to him, which outcome would be worse: If he replied, or if he did not? How could she know? She was only part Irish, and her crystal ball was permanently in for repairs.

Rose dithered, decided to write him, but did not. Weeks went by, until one day she read a magazine story about a woman in her sixties who had gotten up the nerve to ask a man on a date. Not something women of her generation did in their youth, but times had changed. It was obvious the story was based on life. Everything, right down to the floral print on the character's tights, was exact, was lived in. And it ended miserably, no surprise. But still, it happened, it counted, it was real. Rose was ready for real. She had seen enough of life slip by in quarantine. She did not want to envy a character in a magazine. She stopped dithering and sent Mr. Evaporating Eros her phone number.

Two hours later her cell phone rang. Their first call was the kind of chatter you might expect from a pair of nerds. Space flight. States of matter. Evolution. Rose paced her living room, phone in hand, nervous about this crazy kind of rehearsal for a blind date. His name was Brendan, and he talked about neoteny, the evolutionary pressure to retain juvenile traits into adulthood. "The interesting thing is that during domestication, traits that make dogs look more juvenile prevailed independently from behaviors that actually made dogs useful to humans."

This was right up Rose's alley. "Exactly! And that same selective pressure happened to Mickey Mouse. In his first movie, Mickey had a long rat-like snout, but over time his features became rounder and more juvenile. It's de-evolution." She laughed. "Just like that eighties band, Devo."

"Indeed," he said, "And the same process of retaining juvenile traits happened with humans ourselves."

"Including human behavior. Humans are the only apes who play all our lives. Hence the popularity of plastic dinosaurs." She didn't mention her living room décor. Just as well to save that for later.

"Right," he said, "Listen, I need to go. But speaking of dinosaurs, the Academy of Sciences is open for date night on Thursday. Lots of fossils will be there, including me. Meet me there?"

"Alright. I will."

* * *

Rose knew herself to be a natural skeptic. So how did she change from skepticism to suspending her disbelief about this man? It began with trusting where no trust was warranted.

They met in Golden Gate Park at the door of the museum and walked in together. She mentioned she had just crossed the bridge from Berkeley. "We could have driven together," he said. "I drove across from El Cerrito."

"But I don't know you, so I don't know whether that would have been safe."

"Oh," he said, matter-of-factly. "If I wanted to kill you, you'd already be dead."

She was taken aback, but then, he seemed so benign. His Santa Claus look was just not menacing. Brendan had dressed carefully in khaki slacks and a muted green Hawaiian shirt. He looked like Santa on summer vacation. He was a portly man. No way to tell how strong he was, but Rose was sure she could outrun him.

They started the evening on a bench by the *T. Rex* at the entry of the museum. Rose loved that *Rex*, loved its big teeth and its deep eye sockets and its outstretched ribcage. She loved how it was built for speed and for the kill. And it was blessedly silent, while Brendan just kept talking, moving his big fleshy lips. She found herself tuning in and out.

"It was around that time I invented a mammography machine, not the one in use today, unfortunately. Mine was much easier on the breasts." He took her hands in his. It was the first time a man had held her hands in, what? Ten years?

"You know, Rose, I'm very fussy about women. I haven't dated anyone in six months. But I'd really like to see you again." How could she doubt it when he held her hands that way?

That night they spent more time sitting on benches than touring the museum. He told her the fascinating things he had done, dropping the names of half the famous scientists and writers of the twentieth century. And the flattery: "We are so alike, you and I," he said. He would finish her sentences and then say, "You have no idea how close we are, already."

After that night, he sent long emails every day, full of quotations. "Love looks not with the eyes but with the mind," he quoted the Bard. "I would not wish any companion in the world but you." A week later, he came to her door with flowers and swept her off to dinner in his Mercedes. A rather beat-up Mercedes, she noticed, feeling guilty for minding.

After dinner she stood with him on the sidewalk outside the café and he pulled her toward him by her jacket. He kissed her until she had to sit down because her knees refused to keep working. She sat in his car and kissed him and told him about her long-ago marriage to a vegetarian, and he told her that must have been tough because she kissed like a carnivore. And she did kiss like that, with him.

He paused and looked at her. "You do realize sex evolved from animals eating each other."

"Very true." She knew that, but she didn't know anything about this feeling. It was as if she had been a walking Christmas tree all her life and somebody finally plugged the lights into the wall.

A week later she walked down the hall at the lab, heels clicking nervously on the linoleum, knowing she was going to see him that night. Her stomach fluttered as if she were about to be eaten by a large friendly animal. She felt like a willing sacrifice. Or like she was covered in glow paint and if somebody turned off the overhead lights they could read by her. She looked in the mirror at her wrinkles and her greying hair and her goofy grin and thought, *this is what turned on looks like.*

That night on their third date he said, "We are well matched, lovely Rose-with-no-thorns. You and I are so alike that our marriage would be illegal except in Arkansas." She did not know whether to be flattered or just amused that he brought up marriage so soon. He was clearly besotted by charms of which she herself was unaware. She was much better at keeping her head than he was at keeping his.

"You're in hot pursuit," she said. "Why don't you let me chase you for a while?"

But instead, he told Rose that he would support her if she wanted to retire early.

"Good heavens, man! We've known each other for, what, a month?"

"Not a problem," he said, "I've got it socked away. What else am I going to do with it?"

"Brendan, thank you, really. When I'm ready to retire, I will have a university pension. But you're very kind." Only later did she wonder what he would have done, had she called his bluff. A man who drove a dented Mercedes and wore clothes made in the last century could be eccentric, or he could be flat out broke.

The next week they attended a lecture on toxoplasmosis, a parasite that lives in the brains of rodents and dulls their fear of felines.

"It's a strange and wonderful thing," Brendan said, "the love of a mouse for a cat." She shivered at that. Afterwards, Brendan and Rose parked at the crest of the Berkeley hills with a view of the San Francisco Bay. He talked away. She could see from the passenger seat that Brendan's Mercedes was missing a side view mirror. Why would a guy with a pile of money drive around that way? She focused her wandering mind as he said, "After the third marriage, I waited a decade to ponder what I had done wrong. By then I knew I had done nothing wrong." Was he being ironic? Or was he just completely unaware?

Ah, but then, the kisses were lovely.

A week later he invited her to dinner at his house in El Cerrito, north of Berkeley. Brendan lived in a midcentury ranch style, the interior reminiscent of a second-hand electronics store. Dusty gadgets were stacked in every corner. The two of them sat on Brendan's couch, plates of steak on the coffee table in front of them.

"It's challenging to live alone, isn't it, Rose? Even now, when we can move more freely. At least your daughter and granddaughter live nearby. I'm sure that, like me, you've practiced the Heimlich maneuver for one, and picked out a table with a corner at the right height, just in case you ever need it. Morbid, perhaps, but we don't want to give up eating steak, just because we live alone."

Rose swallowed carefully. "I never thought about that. But you're right. Living alone does have its risks."

"Perhaps at some point we could join forces." He kissed her again, one of those big-lipped kisses she was coming to adore. He took his time. She loved it. After running away from sex all her life, she had come home to her body with this man.

Jeopardy was on the television. He fed her bites of filet mignon and answered every question before the contestants could open their mouths. One question stumped him. He looked at her with big serious eyes and said, "Sometimes I don't know these," as if admitting a *faux pas*. He gave her sips of champagne and kissed her in between.

There were things about Brendan that baffled or annoyed her, but she loved the feel of his lips. All tension disappeared when his lips grazed her face, her neck. It was mesmerizing, being kissed like that. It had been years, if ever, since she had been so thoroughly kissed. She floated on a sea of endorphins.

Then somehow the television was off and so was her shirt and then her bra, his beard scratching her breasts, his mouth and teeth pulling hard at her nipples, just hard enough, how did he know? Well of course he knew physiology, and then she thought that every woman in the world should have the chance to make love with a doctor.

It felt like he was everywhere, biting her neck so that the hairs on her arms stood at attention, sliding his hand into the waistband of her pants. She tried to reciprocate, running her fingers down his back, but he did not seem interested, so intent was he on what she was feeling. And what she felt was so enormous, so deafening, that she could barely do anything. She panted, she cried out. There was no sound she could make that would release this feeling.

And then, abruptly, he was standing on the far side of the room.

"Would you be more comfortable in a robe?" he asked, conversationally. "You'd look cute in this one. It's been in the back of my closet forever—some long-ago visitor left it there." Her logical mind was sufficiently aware to realize she was part of a ritual, not a ritual sacrifice, but ritual lovemaking. She nodded, and he helped her to stand, and then helped her out of her clothes and into a silky beige robe. She wondered vaguely whether he washed it since its last occupant, but frankly she didn't care. He put on a bigger gown and they sat back on the couch, and then he really was everywhere, touching her on and in every surface.

"Come to my bed," he said at last.

She followed him into his bedroom, which was full of computer gear, a red light blinking on the computer on his desk. Only the bed itself was clear. In the middle of a heavy gray comforter was a single large Chinese character.

"What does this mean, this symbol on your bedspread?"

"It's the character for wisdom. Beautiful, isn't it? And it suits us both so well, my dear. I've never known anyone like you. So very wise."

They barely slept that night. His beard and his mustache seemed to live between her legs. She cried out in bliss again and again and looked up when he paused to see his bright blue eyes assessing his effect on her.

In the morning they showered together, and he rubbed soapy bellies with her, back and forth like seals playing. Afterwards he blow-dried her hair, and she was laughing, and he said, "Do you feel loved?"

"Yes," said Rose. "Yes, I do."

If it had just stopped there, she thought later. *If I had never expected anything more, I would have been happy.*

But she did expect more, and in a different way, so did he.

[4]

ROSE'S TALE

Everything was alive: books and windows, chairs and tables, inhabited by some force that made them pulse with life. Rose met her daughter for lunch and when she turned the handle of the restaurant door, Linda said, "I can tell you are in love by the way you touch that door." Her nights with Brendan had done this for Rose, had connected her with everything around her. And not just everything outside her—she was alive to herself in a new way.

She tried to tell Brendan, late one night in his bedroom. "You've changed my life. I hope you know that."

He stopped kissing her neck and sat up to look at her. "As a physician, my knowledge of female anatomy is exquisite. I'll grant you that. But I didn't change your life, you did. Your passion belongs to you."

"If it's mine, then why didn't I feel it before? I'm 64 years old and nobody has ever made me feel like this."

"It's your time to bloom. If you hadn't met me, somebody else would have brought this out in you."

"How do you know that?"

"I just do. And anyway, it's only sex. Nice but not necessary.

Don't make the mistake of confusing ice cream with oxygen." He resumed his kisses, his full lips bringing her alive.

"Ice cream. I do love ice cream." She caressed the folds of flesh on his back. His lips slid down to the most sensitive place on her neck, and her glance fell on the red light blinking atop his computer. What was that, anyway? Who knew? Who cared? His lips and his fingers were once again the center of her world. Only one thing concerned her.

"Brendan," she said, breaking her concentration.

"Mmm?"

"Why have you never made love to me?"

"I thought I was."

"You know what I mean. I love everything we do, but we've never..."

"Had penis-in-vagina intercourse? PIV, as the kids call it?"

"Yes. That."

"All in good time, my dear. Patience is a virtue."

He poured her tea the next morning. "It's so rare to meet someone I can really connect with. Someone who is truly from my tribe. I love that we can talk about evolution: how it's smart and stupid, at the same time."

"Exactly! Enough mistakes over millions of years can solve lots of problems." Rose adored their alternating focus on sex and science.

"Just so. And the solutions to those problems vary, depending on circumstance. Take photosynthesis: Different depending on climate."

"Yes, the plants with purple leaves came first. The pigment protects the plants from too much sun. So maybe the world was sunnier when they evolved."

"That could be." Brendan looked thoughtful.

Rose set down her teacup. "And the same problem is solved in desert plants by opening their pores to take in carbon dioxide only at night."

"Oh really? That's interesting. I wonder how the biotech people are exploiting that."

"Maybe they're not."

"Indeed. Maybe not."

* * *

Brendan dearly loved to talk about photosynthesis. Rose's research focused on vertebrate evolution, but she began to study up on plants so she could tell him new things. Later it embarrassed her that she had lent Brendan her mind along with her body, but at least her students got the benefit of what she learned.

She added a new lecture to the curriculum for her sophomores. It began with a diagram of the environmental cycle between photosynthesis and respiration: Sunlight shining on plants and animals. At the bottom of the screen was the English version of the equation for photosynthesis.

Carbon dioxide + water + energy from sunlight yields glucose and oxygen.

Onstage, Rose put on her headset microphone, picked up her laser pointer, and glanced at the screen overhead. Her career began in the blackboard era, but these days she was decked out as if she were giving a TED talk. She spent her lectures clicking through slide decks, keeping things moving at a pace that held the interest of the swipe-left generation.

Rose told them, "Our lives are built around cycles: Winter and Summer, day and night, and the intimate cycle of our breath."

Do not mention sex, she told herself. *Do. Not.*

"We breathe in oxygen from plants and breathe out carbon dioxide. And plants, in turn, take in carbon dioxide, water, and sunlight, and break up carbon dioxide to give us oxygen, while they store energy in sugars made with carbon. That process in plants—photosynthesis—is the most important chemical reaction on earth. The balance between plants and animals underlies all of life. But keep in mind that plants alone can perform both sides of the process. Plants would do just fine without us, but we would be dead without plants."

Rose clicked to the next slide showing the conversion of plankton to fossil fuels. "Over millions of years, as tiny plants called phytoplankton died in the oceans, geological pressure turned their stored energy into fossil fuels: oil and gas. When we burn fossil fuels, we release a lot of carbon dioxide, and throw off that cycle we all depend on. We change what the air is made of, and the planet heats up. Relying on fossil fuels is a mistake that seemed like a good idea at the time. We all make those mistakes, don't we?"

Her last line earned a few knowing murmurs from the students. And with that, Isis raised her hand in the front row of the lecture hall.

"Yes, Isis?"

"Are there ways to fix this extra carbon dioxide problem? To strengthen the photosynthesis side of the cycle?"

Rose was impressed. "That's a key question. Plants only store a small portion of sunlight as energy, so there is much room for improvement. A lot more carbon dioxide could be stored away. Maybe some of you will work on that someday. I hope so."

* * *

After several months of naked botany, Rose and Brendan took a trip up the California coast to Mendocino. It was billed as a romantic weekend away, but Brendan took the opportunity to grill Rose about the unique flora of the town and its environs. Manzanita, cypress, and flowering aster, all have types that only grow on the Mendocino peninsula. "And what about that *Cuscuta pacifica*, eh?" He pointed it out happily. "The *papillata* variety only grows here! Pretty great, huh?"

Rose relaxed while he drove, her sunglasses filtering out the glare while she took in the sights. "Let me guess: You spent last evening looking up the plants in this area, and now you hope you know more local trivia than the biologist."

He frowned. "Hah! You know me too well."

Perhaps she did.

B rendan had booked a room at a bed and breakfast, one of the restored Victorian homes that dot the Mendocino coast. It was run by a couple in their seventies named George and Betty. Rose imagined without any data that the two of them had been happily married for fifty years. She suddenly realized she had never slept in a hotel with a man who was not her husband. Was it her imagination or did Betty look at her knowingly while she checked them in? After all, neither Rose nor Brendan wore a wedding ring. George insisted on carrying their bags upstairs, although he was older than they were. He set the bags down in their room. "I hope you and your wife have a nice stay."

"I'm sure we will," said Brendan.

Their room faced inland, toward the hills not the sea, which was too bad; but they were just a two-block walk from the cliffs and inlets that made this stretch of coastline memorable. As they walked along the bluffs that afternoon, Brendan said, "Since I'm picking up the hotel, it seems reasonable for you to pay the dinner tab."

"Sure, I'd be glad to do that."

"Great! I've made a reservation at my favorite place."

Rose hoped he kept in mind that she was on a professor's salary, but that night, as they walked into The Justinian, she realized Brendan had chosen the only Michelin five-star restaurant in town.

Its cozy interior, reminiscent of places she had visited on the coast of Maine, was impeccably maintained. But at those prices it should be.

Once seated, Brendan was laser focused on the menu. "As I recall, their oysters are superb."

"I despise oysters."

"Ah! More for me, then." He looked up at Rose for an instant, then continued perusing the heavy menu, hung with gold braid and a tassel.

"Hello, I'm Brandy. I'll be your server this evening." Their waitress was barely twenty, the age of Rose's students, and had the sun-kissed look of blonde white girls who grow up by the sea. Brendan looked Brandy up and down with a hungry gaze. "I'll have the oysters to start. And how about you?" He gave Rose a quick glance.

"I'm fine for now. I'll just have a main course, thank you."

She was not surprised when Brendan followed up his oysters with the second most expensive entrée and the second priciest dessert on the menu, all accompanied by a full bottle of the second most expensive wine. He beamed at her. "After all, we don't need to drive anywhere, do we?"

Rose did not bother objecting. She could predict he would have gone full indignation mode and pointed out that, after all, he hadn't ordered the most expensive items. Why go through that charade?

Back in their hotel room, Brendan took his time in the bathroom and ran the tap for several minutes. He came out in a bathrobe, climbed into bed with her, and said, "This is your lucky night."

"Why? Because you'll think about Brandy while you make love to me?"

He chuckled. "From your standpoint, isn't that better than if I thought about you while making love to Brandy?"

Still smiling, Brendan turned out the light. He opened his robe and lay his massive bulk on top of her. "Foreplay is overrated, don't you think?"

So that is what he meant by "lucky night." She would have reached down to stroke his cock, but his gut was in the way. He parted her legs and slid into her, and in spite of being annoyed with him, Rose realized she was aroused enough by Brendan's skin and his kisses that his deep penetration was exquisite. The feeling of him inside her was just bliss. His cock seemed to rub and catch on her vulva in a different way than any sex she could remember. It felt so fantastic that she forgot about Brendan's flirtation with Brandy. She forgot about the expense of dinner and the knowing wink from Betty when they arrived back at the inn. She forgot to worry about the guests in the next room and called out sounds of passion as if they were at home. She forgot everything but her own rapture. Then she slept, hard and deep.

Rose woke to the full light of morning. Seagulls circled in the blue sky out the window. She could hear murmurs of conversation and the clink of glassware from guests having breakfast on the patio. Brendan was already up and showering. His side of the bed was still warm. She reached under his pillow to pull it toward her. There was something under his pillow: something stiff and cylindrical, with a rough, nubby texture. She lifted the pillow and looked. It was a rubber phallus about eight inches long with one flat end. And in the flat end was a hole, about the circumference of a thumb.

[5]

THE PILLOW TALKS

Back at The Lab, Joyce almost jumped from her chair. "No way! Are you fucking kidding?"

Maxine looked thoughtful. "That explains a lot. He spent so much time in the bathroom at night with the water running."

Rose was embarrassed. "That was an overshare, wasn't it? I'm sorry, I just met you..."

"Not at all. I'd rather know," said Maxine. "That's why we're here."

Joyce simmered down. "If he had said something it would be different. If he had been upfront and explained why he needed to use it and asked for consent. It's the lying that's infuriating. What was he doing all that time in the bathroom? Applying some kind of adhesive?"

Maxine shook her head. "Seems likely, but at this point who cares? Rose, tell what happened next."

"OK. I was so shocked by the thing under the pillow that I didn't know what to say. So I said nothing. I kept glancing over as we packed to see if he'd try to sneak it into his overnight bag. But he didn't. He must have thought he'd packed it earlier, while I was still asleep. As we left the room, I kept wondering what the housekeepers would think when they changed the sheets."

Maxine laughed and launched into an old song with a new twist. "I left my... dick..."

Joyce joined in, "...in Mendocino..."

"Shh! People are staring at us!" Rose was aghast.

"Keep talking, Rose! What happened next? Not that anything could top that." Maxine suppressed her laughter and put on her best serious lawyer face.

* * *

S tunned as she was by the discovery of his appliance, Rose said nothing to Brendan as they finished packing. She was quiet as they drove south.

Brendan did not seem to notice. "I'm off to a consulting gig in San Diego today. When we get to my place, let's switch to your car and you can drop me off at the Oakland Airport. Does that work?"

"Alright, Brendan. I can do that." In that moment Rose could not muster much enthusiasm for an extra hour with Brendan.

She remained quiet the rest of the drive, and he easily filled the silence, pontificating about solar power, the evolution of parasites, and the likely source of the next pandemic. The view out the window transformed as they drove south, from coastal forest to the vineyards of the wine country, and on to the Marin cities. They drove over the San Rafael bridge with its wide views of the bay and San Francisco. They left Brendan's car at his house and both climbed into Rose's minivan. Brendan gave her a peck on the cheek when she dropped him off at the airport curb with his overnight bag of dirty clothes.

As she drove away, Rose glanced back at him in the rearview mirror. Brendan did not walk into the airport. He did not act like somebody who was getting on a flight. Instead, he stood at the curb in his Panama hat, looking at the traffic. As she lost sight of Brendan, a car was just slowing in front of him. The driver appeared to be a Caucasian woman with greying auburn hair.

Brendan called less often after that. But when he did call, he acted like nothing was wrong. They would still get together and talk science, especially botany. He might serve hamburger instead of steak, and the vegetables might not be fresh, but he still had her over for dinner.

"Is it true that some forms of algae are actually bacteria, and aren't plants at all?" Brendan asked one night between bites of canned pork and beans.

"Yes." Rose was trying to eat what he served but was glad to put down her fork. "Algae is a catch-all term for various organisms. But almost all of them photosynthesize, mostly using chlorophyl, that absorbs all visible light except green."

"Which is why plants look green."

"That's right. But one group of algae, called the cryptophytes, absorbs a huge range of wavelengths, way beyond the visible spectrum. That makes them extra efficient at photosynthesis."

Brendan looked interested. "What color are they?"

"I'm not sure, actually."

"Why don't you order some and find out? You do have a research budget, right?"

"My budget is for my own projects. I research vertebrates. I'm not a plant biologist."

"You are now."

Rose had a hard time sleeping that night, while Brendan snored gently into his CPAP. She got out of his bed and put on the silk robe that Brendan said some long-ago visitor left there. The tie was just where it should be—it was so slippery it sometimes slid out of its loops, so Rose had tied knots at the loops on her previous visit. Now she reached into the silky pocket and found a folded slip of paper. By the bathroom light she opened it and read: *Illegitimi non carborundum.*

Quietly, she slid the paper into her backpack and looked up the phrase on her phone. It was pig Latin:

Don't let the bastards grind you down.

"**D**o you want breakfast?" Brendan asked in the morning. He bustled about the kitchen in his big blue kimono, getting the coffee started.

"No thanks. I need to get to campus. But I do have a question."

"Yes?" He glanced up from the stove.

"Do you go out with other women?"

"That's not what you really mean, is it, Rose? You want to know if I go *in* with other women." His joke clearly amused him. "And the answer is no. It's not a moral issue for me. It's simply a matter of focus. When I'm with a woman I'm with her. I have woman friends, of course. Women are my favorite people. But so much of my energy is focused on my work, I can only manage one relationship at a time."

She thought about showing him the slip of paper from the robe. But what would be the point?

* * *

Two weeks later, Rose was driving Ella and her friends to baseball practice. Rose was happy that her minivan was back in chauffeur service, now the pandemic was over. Ella was in the passenger seat and three of her teammates were in back, all in blue uniforms with yellow numbers. Driving these girls was one of Rose's favorite grandma duties. It took her mind off the weeks when she did not see Brendan, and the times when he was with her but his mind seemed elsewhere. Instead, she got to concentrate on her grand-daughter.

"Nona?" Ella asked, sounding shy.

"Yes, Ell?"

"We were wondering..." Ella's voice was much quieter than usual.

"What is it? Spit it out, child. You know you can ask me anything."

Ella spoke up a bit, loud enough for the girls in the back seat to hear. "OK. Did Mom tell you we've been taking Sex Ed at school?"

So it was that kind of question. Rose steeled herself. "I didn't know that, but good for you. That's great."

Ella continued. "They tell us some stuff, but one thing they didn't tell us is..."

In the back seat, all three girls giggled. Clearly they knew what Ella was about to ask.

"What is it?"

Ella took the plunge. "What happens when guys ejaculate? I mean, how far does it go?"

Rose laughed. "What a question! You *are* growing up, aren't you?"

Ella shrugged. "Maybe."

Rose put on her best professorial voice. "Well, it depends. If you're talking about teenagers, college boys have contests to see who can hit the ceiling."

Squeals and giggles came from the back seat. Ella turned red.

"But by the time they're seventy, they burble like broken drinking fountains." Rose sounded serious now, and maybe a little bitter. The giggling stopped and the girls in the back said, "Ewww."

Ella looked at her grandmother. "Nona."

"Yes, dear?"

"How do you know that? About the seventy-year-olds?"

Rose regained her professional composure. "I'm a biologist. We know these things."

Ella paused. "Mom told me you've been seeing someone."

"That wasn't her news to share."

"Are you having fun?"

Fun. No, Rose was not having much fun. Not with Brendan, not any more. "I'm enjoying being with you and your friends, dear. Driving you to practice like this is fun."

"That's not what I mean."

Rose paused. "I'm fine. I'll be fine. And I'm always happy to see you."

After practice, Rose took Ella home and stayed for dinner. Rose and Linda cleaned up the kitchen afterwards.

Linda looked serious. "Mom?"

"Yes, dear?"

"Thanks for driving the girls today."

"It's my pleasure. It really is, you know. I'm not just saying that."

"I'm glad. Listen, Ella told me about your conversation."

"Oh. I hope it wasn't inappropriate. The girls did ask a very direct question."

"Really? She didn't talk about that part. She just said she doesn't think you're happy in your dating life. So I wanted to say I'm sorry for suggesting you set up a profile. Maybe it was a mistake."

"Perhaps. But not all mistakes are bad." Rose rinsed a platter and stacked it by the sink.

"Yeah, I know." Linda quoted something she had heard from her mother since childhood: "If it weren't for mistakes, we'd still be slime mold."

"Actually, we wouldn't have made it that far. Not even to single cells. But seriously, I don't think this relationship has been such a mistake. Women get stronger with age. You remember how I struggled when your dad left. Even though we weren't right for each other, and I knew it. But that was a different part of my life. When you're really a grownup, you can do the dishes just fine with a broken heart."

Linda remembered those tough times years earlier, after her dad left, when her mother pulled it together to comfort her but then cried quietly in her adjoining bedroom. She wiped the suds off her hands and hugged Rose. "From now on, if you are going to date, find a guy who worships the ground you walk on."

"I thought I had." Rose sounded rueful.

Just then Rick walked into the kitchen with a stack of dirty plates. "Poor Rose. Sat on Santa's lap so many times and never got what she wanted."

"But I did," said Rose. "For a while."

[6]

HER FAVORITE MISTAKE

Rose always wore her lab coat to lecture. After decades on the Cal Berkeley faculty, the coat still gave her confidence a boost. A woman in front of the lecture hall could be some grandmother going back for her degree, but a woman in a white coat looked authoritative—and smart.

But how smart am I, Rose wondered, *to keep seeing Brendan Burns?* She checked her dark hair in the front hall mirror and pushed Brendan from her thoughts. Today she was teaching, not brooding.

Rose enjoyed the twenty-minute walk from her bungalow to the University of California. She crossed Oxford Street to the stand of redwood trees that marked the edge of campus. Her face bare, she inhaled the cool foggy air off the San Francisco Bay. After the pandemic, Rose would never again take fresh air for granted. As she waved to other faculty across a green lawn, she felt so free. It was far different from how she felt in her relationship.

When she first met Brendan, Rose could not believe her luck. He was smart, engaging, enticing. A year later, as she got to know the man behind the façade, she suspected dating Brendan was a big mistake. That was not necessarily a bad thing. *After all*, she reminded herself as she neared the Life Sciences Building, *if you're around long enough to make lots of mistakes, some turn out to be great. Mistakes gave us the dinosaurs.* That was exactly what Rose was about to tell her students.

Rose entered the paneled hall through the professor's back door and walked onto the lecture platform. She looked out at a hundred bright young faces in ascending rows. So wonderful to see their range of ethnicities and genders. Decades earlier, when Rose joined the faculty, it was rare for any woman—even a white woman like her—to teach science at a major university. But when it came time for Rose to retire, she hoped her successor would reflect the rainbow in front of her. These science majors were eager to learn what she had to offer: genetics, evolution, and a bit of home-grown wisdom. *There is a reason why women live way past menopause, unlike most female mammals,* Rose thought. *By this age, we know a thing or two. Or so we hope.* Rose clicked past the title screen to today's first slide, a professional-looking animation that showed DNA creating RNA on the way to making protein.

"Good afternoon." Rose's amplified voice rang out across the hall. Stragglers hastily found seats and opened their laptops to take notes. A hundred students fixed their collective gaze on the petite dark-haired woman in horn rim glasses on the raised stage.

"Today we'll review how life makes life, and discuss how mistakes are key to that process. Remember that DNA is the backup copy for all the information needed to make a living thing. Opening the DNA library and making a working copy on RNA is called *transcription.*" Rose laser-pointed at the word on the screen. "And the cell does it perfectly, nine hundred and ninety-nine times out of a thousand."

Rose advanced to the next slide and pointed to *translation* on the screen. The slide showed RNA codon triplets binding amino acids.

"After transcription, RNA *translates* the sequence into amino acids, the building blocks of *protein*, which is what we are made of. Again, the cell does this right, almost all the time. But not always, thank goodness."

Marisol Sanchez raised her hand. She was a curvy Biology major who favored hoop earrings and asked great questions. Rose knew the names of twenty or so in this room, the students who asked the most questions.

"Yes, Marisol?"

"Dr. Bingham, wouldn't it be better if our genes did it right every time?"

Rose smiled. "You would think so, wouldn't you? A genetic mistake can be a big problem for a living thing. But not always—mistakes have various outcomes." Rose mentally thanked Marisol—she could not have asked for a better segue. She clicked to a slide with the matrix of codes that genes use to translate RNA to protein. "Each RNA codon includes three letters from a four-letter alphabet, so there are 64 possible codons, and just twenty amino acids. So, there are multiple versions of the three-letter nucleic acid codes, or *codons*, that match each of the twenty amino acids. They're redundant. Synonyms, they would say in the English department."

Rose pointed to an example. "This kind of mistake makes no difference at all. Imagine there are two cartons of pasteurized whole milk in your fridge, and you use your roommate's by mistake. Your roommate might not like it, but your cereal would taste the same."

Next Rose pointed out a codon that tells RNA to stop coding. "But other mistakes create nonsense. They make a protein that is too short, because the code says to stop in the middle of a protein. Or they make proteins that just don't work. Those mistakes are like pouring spoiled milk on your cereal. They shut everything down. Most errors kill the organism or cause life-changing illness, like cystic fibrosis."

Rose clicked to the next slide, an amphibian leaving the ocean and breathing air. "But every once in a while, a mistake leads to some-thing new, something even better. That kind of mistake is like pouring chocolate milk on your cereal and discovering it's delicious. Those mistakes make magic happen."

The next slide showed the Tree of Life, each branch representing a major class of living beings. There were worms, trees, primates, bacteria. "Every form of life — every flower, every animal — is alive because of mistakes that worked — mistakes that opened up possibilities. Beneficial mistakes give animals longer coats during an ice age. Enough beneficial mistakes can create something new, like the first animal to emerge from sea to land. Or like the dinosaurs. If it weren't for good mistakes, we wouldn't even be slime mold."

Good mistakes. At first it had been so good. An image came to Rose's mind: she and Brendan naked in bed, his hands on her skin, his eyes locked on her face, gauging his effect on her. *Dr. Bingham!* she told herself. *Stop. Get a grip.*

Just then Isis raised her hand.

"Yes, Isis?"

"So, changes in environment favor some mistakes. But what about the changes we humans want? What about how farmers breed plants and animals?"

Rose smiled. "That's a great question! Because it's exactly what we'll talk about next!" A few students chuckled. "Humans have been directing evolution for domestic plants and animals for thousands of years. And we still do it the old-fashioned way, by selective breeding. Think about seedless watermelons, or wiener dogs bred to hunt badgers. But these days there are better tools."

Rose clicked to a diagram of bacterial gene splicing, with the molecular "scissors" and "glue" that were the first inventions of biotechnology. "We have enzymatic tools that open bacterial DNA and let us splice in the directions for proteins we want, like the medicines created by biotechnology. That whole industry is built on intentional mistakes. It's like convincing your roommate to pour malt powder and ice cream into his milk and then give you the carton of milkshake. Wouldn't that be fabulous?"

Rose glanced at the clock on the back wall as the students murmured polite amusement.

Rose waved at them. "I've kept you overtime. Thank you all for your focus. That's it for today."

They gathered their things, talking with animation. She had given them something to think about. Good.

As the rest of the students filed out of the hall, Marisol climbed the steps to the lecture platform, her backpack slung on one shoulder. "Thanks, Dr. Bingham. You make biology so interesting."

Rose shook her head. "It's not me. What could be more interesting than life itself?"

Marisol nodded. "I mean, it's great you have such enthusiasm, at your age."

Rose was not in the habit of rolling her eyes, but right then she was tempted. "Your sixties will come along, Marisol—sooner than you expect. Young people get older, that's how it works."

"I know..." Marisol looked embarrassed.

"We're not insects, born to live out predetermined programs. Humans grow and learn for decades, in different ways, depending on our interests. Here's the key: Find something that thrills you and then do it. You'll have passion your whole life." *If you're lucky,* thought Rose. *If you don't waste your passion on someone who doesn't deserve it.*

"Hey, I'm sorry if I offended you."

"Not at all, Marisol. When I was your age, I had no idea what life had to offer past forty. Just be kind to your future self. And don't be afraid to take chances and make mistakes. Here, I'll walk you out. We can use the professor's door."

Rose locked up the lecture hall and set off to see Brendan, her chosen mistake. What was that choice about? Why pour spoiled milk on the cereal of life? Wasn't her logical mind in charge of her decisions? No, apparently not.

As Rose walked home, the thought of Brendan lightened her step. In the battle between logic and lust, she knew which part of her brain was winning.

Tonight Brendan Burns, the object of her desire, was coming to dinner.

* * *

The light from the big windows in the bar was fading as Rose neared the end of her story. While she was talking, Maxine had ordered appetizers for the table. She and Joyce chewed crudités in silence while Rose finished her story.

"I hadn't seen Brendan in two weeks. I sent him an email saying we should talk — and he sent me that Pablo Neruda email. We agreed he would come to my house for dinner. But we didn't talk, not really. Then we got in bed naked and he turned over and started reading. I tried to get his attention and he told me it was unseemly for me to be interested in sex at my age. He went to sleep but I couldn't. I got up and washed the dishes, and then he got up, and walked out without logging out of his emails on my computer. And that's when I found the two of you."

"Wow." For once, the articulate Maxine was almost speechless.

"What an asshole." Joyce said it like she meant it.

Maxine sat up tall. "Damn straight. I barely know you, Rose, but I am sure you deserve better."

Joyce thought back. "And to top it off, while all that was happening, Brendan and I started dating. I met Brendan online a few months after you did, Rose. Courtesy of my husband."

"Your *what?*" Rose was stunned.

So was Maxine. "Oh, now, wait a minute."

[7]

JOYCE'S TALE

Gary and Joyce Farrell owned a comfortable ranch style house, vintage 1970, in the Richmond hills north of El Cerrito. One Saturday night the two of them talked while Joyce made dinner. Gary leaned over the kitchen island. His blonde hair had gone white, but he retained the lanky frame that first attracted Joyce in their college days.

"Let's plan a dinner party of vaccinated friends," said Joyce.

"All our friends are vaccinated, but let's not invite them all at once. How about the couples with the prettiest wives?"

"Is that a joke? I'm not sure it's funny."

Joyce loved Gary and was sure Gary loved her. But they had been married forty years, and Joyce knew in the back of her mind that her husband was "antsy," as she called it. He watched more porn lately and gazed with longing at women they passed on the street. But she did not know what was really on his mind, not until that night.

"Listen, Joyce."

"Yes?"

"You're the light of my life and that will never change. Ever. You were also my first love, and sometimes I wonder..." He looked down.

"What do you wonder, Gary?"

"I wonder what it would be like to be with a different woman. I wonder how it would be if we opened our marriage."

Joyce started to answer, but Gary held up his hand.

"Just to be clear, Joyce, I only want this if it's mutual. I'm interested in some variety but only if it's alright with you. And our marriage would always come first. Will you think about it?"

At that moment Joyce was stirring a pan of hot gravy. She picked up the pan, walked over to her husband and poured gravy on his shoes.

They avoided the subject of open marriage after that. But the more Joyce thought about it, the more reasonable it seemed. Joyce had enjoyed plenty of chances to sow wild oats at the technical college they both attended, which had just gone coed back in the seventies and was mostly men. Those odds had not been in Gary's favor, and he was inexperienced when they met; no wonder he was curious now. If they opened their marriage, they would still be together. Gary would get the variety he craved, and Joyce could have adventures too, if she wished. It would not be a free-for-all, just a different set of agreements. After pondering for several months, Joyce sat down with Gary in their living room and let him know she was ready to give it a try.

Gary would not soon forget the Night of the Hot Gravy. "Are you sure, Joyce? I thought you hated the idea. Polyamory isn't what you signed up for when we married."

"I don't want you to feel trapped. That's why I'm at least willing to try it out. But if we're going to open our marriage, it needs to be open for both of us. I won't sit home while you go out on the town. That's not my style."

Gary was eager to help. "Sure, I support that. You know how people find each other these days, with dating profiles." He opened his laptop. "Here's an example. This service helps you find compatible people. People with whom you'll have chemistry."

Joyce didn't laugh. "Yet another joke about me being a chemist."

"Can't help it." Gary was smiling; Joyce was not.

She checked out the screen. "Are you on this website?"

"I built a profile, but I didn't make it active. It was just in case you decided to agree."

Joyce was wistful. "You know if I make a profile, this website is going to tell me to date you."

Gary was too jazzed to hear the plaintive note in his wife's voice. "I'm sure we will run into each other. But you'll have more choices. Hey, check this guy out. He sounds smart. Or at least, *he* thinks he is."

And with that, Gary showed his wife the online profile of a certain Brendan Burns:

Many things fascinate me: How life evolves over time, like a Rube Goldberg machine that builds itself.

Not to mention the biological basis of human love (and how to end human war, given our problematic biology), our connection with the cosmos writ large (and how quantum theory bends that connection), the role of humor in human life, the manifold uses of love poetry, how best to keep passion vivid in long-term love, the future of space travel, and the other life forms we are likely to find on our unfolding sojourn through the universe.

"I'm impressed by the man's ego," said Gary. "You have to meet him and tell me if he's the real thing or a total stuffed shirt."

And so Joyce encountered Brendan, not as a potential lover but as a possible friend with benefits. They had coffee, they got along, she decided he was not a serial killer, and they exchanged vaccination records and the negative results of recent STD tests. Within a week she was standing in his living room. Through the open door of his bedroom she could see the duvet on his bed with its appliquéd Chinese character and the computer with the blinking red light above the monitor.

Brendan was effusive. "Welcome to the Popcorn Palace! Our specialty is romantic comedy, for the woman who doesn't believe in love."

Joyce found this confusing. "You do understand that I'm married, and in an open relationship."

Brendan nodded. "Of course! I respect your honesty, Joyce. And I must be just as honest with you: I could never be anything but monogamous."

"There's no need for that on my account." Joyce was deliberately blunt. "Romance is not my goal here."

"I understand. And I don't think there's anything morally wrong with polyamory. It's just a matter of focus. I've never known anyone like you, so intelligent, so self-confident, and I want nothing more."

"Perhaps getting down to specifics will help. You need to know that I'll spend at least every Thursday through Saturday with my husband Gary. That's our agreement. Plus, I'm in the lab at work a couple evenings a week."

Brendan nodded. "I'll just revert to living like a monk when you're not here. It comes naturally. I'm working on several projects."

"As long as we are honest with one another."

"Indeed. That is essential."

Joyce crossed the room and looked at Brendan's shelves. "You have quite a collection of Star Trek DVDs to keep you company when you're not with friends."

"Yes. I started to download those in my youth, and by now I have almost a full set. Bootleg, of course, but I only watch them alone, so I'm not too far afield from copyright law. But here, come sit with me. I don't bite. At least, not too often." He patted the couch seat beside him.

Once they kissed, Joyce stopped worrying about Brendan becoming emotionally involved. She stopped thinking about anything at all. He was a practiced lover, and he took his time, noticing her most sensitive areas. She had a sudden thought that he had started a new file on her, in that capacious skull of his, but she didn't mind.

Not when the touch of his big bearish hands felt this good. At his suggestion, they doffed their clothes in favor of robes—for him, a blue Japanese print, and he offered her a silky oyster beige.

When next he spoke, in the midst of a caress, she was so deep in reverie that it startled her. "And getting back to my deep respect for your integrity: here's quite a coincidence, Joyce. If I may show you my room. Embroidered on the comforter is a fine example of the Chinese character for honesty."

* * *

"No!" said Maxine. "He told you that character meant honesty? What gall."

"Let her talk," said Rose.

"Uh-huh. And Rose, he told you he was a doctor? He told me that too and I looked him up. He was no such thing."

Rose ignored that for the moment. "What happened next, Joyce?"

* * *

In bed that night, Joyce was mesmerized by Brendan's touch. She expected to find it jarring to touch someone other than Gary after so many years of fidelity, but Brendan drove those thoughts from her mind. As he kissed her inner thighs, she laughed with delight.

"Your beard tickles my thighs."

Brendan paused to look up at her. "And my thoughts tickle your brain. Good arrangement, don't you think?"

After that night, Brendan and Joyce saw each other every Sunday and Tuesday. The arrangement went so well, they started meeting on Wednesdays too. It was a funny thing, Joyce mused, adding another relationship on top of a marriage. It was not quite like dating—or at least, with Brendan it was not. It was more comfortable than that, like adding a parallel marriage with more sex. For a while it seemed too good to be true.

Meanwhile, Joyce's husband Gary met a woman named Pam. Or at least, Joyce thought they had just met, though she sometimes wondered exactly how long they had known one another. Pam invited Joyce to tea at a cozy neighborhood café, and Joyce was curious to meet her.

Pam Gregory turned out to be a fifty-something marketing director at a Berkeley software company. When Joyce caught up with her under an umbrella at an outdoor table, Pam was wearing a dirndl skirt and flat shoes. She was attractive but not too attractive. Her manner was upbeat, whether by nature or in an effort to court the wife's favor, Joyce could not tell.

"I'm a big fan of your marriage." Pam smiled at Joyce as they sat, tea in hand. "I don't want to see Gary more than once or twice a week. And it's clear that he has plenty of passion to share with both of us."

"Thank you, Pam. I'm glad that we both make him happy. He's a good man." It was hard to warm up to this aspect of an open marriage; getting comfortable with taking her own lover was easier. But Pam did seem like a good choice for Gary.

Her husband paced nervously as Joyce walked in the front door that night. "Well? How was it?"

"She seems nice." Joyce was noncommittal yet surprised at how accepting she felt.

"So, are we good to go?"

Joyce smiled. "You have my blessing, Gary."

. . .

It was a giddy next few months. The sex with Brendan was great, and Gary and Joyce had terrific sex too. In fact, it was the best sex with her husband in years. Joyce had feared that his lovemaking with Pam would leave him with little passion for her, but the opposite seemed to be true. Gary came to bed with Joyce alive and eager, his body full of delight, his touch electric. He became as in their early days more lover than husband, exploring her body as if it were new to him, finding fresh ways to bring her joy.

"I love you so much, Gary," Joyce whispered as they drifted to sleep one night.

Gary held her fast in his arms and kissed her. "I'll bet you say that to all the boys."

"No," said Joyce. "Just to you."

[8]
JOYCE STEPS OUT

J oyce waved goodbye to Gary out their living room window one Thursday night, as he left for a date with Pam. Every once in a while their schedules shifted and Gary went out while she was home, but Joyce found she was alright with that. She liked Pam, and she liked how happy her husband was. And it turned out she liked having time on her own. Between her marriage, her workouts at the gym, her trysts with Brendan, and running a lab at work, it was a rare treat to have time to herself. Joyce sat down to read the news but her thoughts turned to the night before with Brendan.

She picked him up at the airport and they had dinner at his place, then watched a movie as usual before going to bed and having sex. Brendan was such a considerate lover, seeming to find his enjoyment in her pleasure. They often had several sexy interludes, interspersed with some of the most erudite conversation Joyce had experienced in bed. Brendan put his big arms around her as they lay naked in his bed that night. "When they talk about screwing each other's brains out, they forget how tough that is for folks like us. Too many neurons."

Joyce smiled. "So it seems."

He propped himself on one elbow. "Tell you what: Let's play Intelligent Design."

"Sounds like a fun game. I'll bite. How does it go?"

"If you were designing photosynthesis from scratch..."

"Photosynthesis?" Joyce was incredulous. "The chemical reaction that turns sunlight into food? The basis for all life on this planet? That's some game!"

Brendan would not be deterred. "...if you were creating photosynthesis, what would you do differently?"

"Seriously? How would I mess with the source of our oxygen, and our energy? Well, first I would choose intermediates that bind more strongly to carbon dioxide."

"Good. Like what?"

"You really want to talk about this now?"

"Yes. Do tell."

She laughed. "You are the biggest nerd."

He saluted. "At your service, Ma'am."

The next few months were a heady time, in bed and out. But by six months in, things began to change. As he served her coffee one morning, Brendan said, "By the way, Joyce, I need to move our Wednesday date to Thursday next week."

Joyce looked at him, annoyed. "I can't do that. You know I spend Thursday nights with Gary."

"Do you? I'd forgotten. Too bad. We'll just see each other two nights next week, then."

Joyce had long wondered about Brendan's claims of a "monk-like existence" when she was not there. Perhaps it was closer to mink-like. "Are you going out with someone else on Wednesday?"

"I'm not going *in* with someone else. And that's what you really mean, isn't it?" By the way he delivered that line, it was clear Brendan had amused himself. Joyce wondered how often he had said it before.

"I just want to understand why we're changing the schedule. You're free to do what you wish, of course."

"Yes, Joyce, you've made that very clear."

Meaning what?

After that, their visits grew more erratic. Sometimes Brendan only gave a day or two notice about changing their plans.

A few weeks later, when Joyce was still annoyed, Brendan said to her, "I've observed you are a bit rigid about when we see each other. We don't need to be joined at the hip. By now we know each other so well, I suspect I know you better than your husband does."

"That's absurd. I've been married to Gary for forty years."

"Yes," said Brendan. "Long enough for him to forget what he thought he knew about you."

A good line, if a bit practiced.

But even though she felt less comfortable, Joyce and Brendan still had some wild nights in bed. And back home, Joyce and Gary did too.

Despite Brendan's claim to the contrary, her husband knew Joyce very well—and he could tell that something was not right.

After they made love one Saturday afternoon, Gary said, "Joyce, how are you doing?"

She was very much in the moment. "Are you kidding? That was great. Yum."

"No, I mean, how are *you* doing? You, Joyce, as a person? Are you OK with how things are going, with us, and with you and Brendan?"

"I love how we're doing. I love how happy you are."

"I am happy. I'm married to the most wonderful woman. The most understanding."

"Thanks, but how understanding would I be, if I weren't with Brendan too? As for Brendan and me—I don't know. There are times when I wonder whether he's being upfront. And sometimes I don't feel respected the way I do with you."

Gary frowned. "Like how?"

"It's his attitude. Like he thinks there is something wrong with me for going outside my marriage."

"Even though he's known all along that you are married and poly."

"Yes, even though. He wasn't like that at first."

Gary shook his head. "If Brendan doesn't make you happy, stop seeing him."

"And then what? Sit around here when I would have been with him?"

"There are lots of fish in the sea, Joyce. Don't settle. I can cut back on seeing Pam if that would make it easier."

Joyce propped up on one muscular arm. "That's sweet of you, Gary, but it's not fair to her. Pam is good to you. We can't treat people like chess pieces. Let's give this Brendan thing a little more time."

"Alright, if you like. I want polyamory to work for both of us."

"I know." But could it work for both of them? Joyce was less sure than she had been at first. Then on a visit to Brendan, Joyce made a discovery.

She was going to take a shower and went to get the silky woman's robe Brendan kept in his closet. She hung it up in the bathroom and realized there were knots tied at the belt loops. This would have been a sensible thing to do, since the belt tended to slip when she wore it. Only she had never tied those knots.

"What is this?" Joyce took the robe out to Brendan, startled.

"What? What's the matter?"

She held out the robe. "How did these knots get here?"

"I could have done that. To keep the tie from falling onto the closet floor."

"You 'could have' done it? What a strange use of the subjunctive. Either you tied the knots or you didn't."

Their eyes met. He said nothing. Joyce took the robe back in the bathroom. She showered, very quietly. Then she wrapped herself in a towel, lifted the robe off the hook and smelled it. Was that the scent of someone else's perfume, or was it her imagination?

By then Brendan was cooking breakfast. She found a slip of paper and wrote on it an old British Intelligence saying in pig Latin that meant, "Don't let the bastards grind you down." She folded the page, slid it into the pocket of the robe and hung it back in the closet.

Joyce collected her hair gel and deodorant from the bathroom, where they had been for months, and put them in her overnight bag. She left nothing behind except her shampoo and conditioner, which were being depleted more rapidly than she would have expected if she were the only one using them.

But she did come back, and the note was gone next time Joyce wore the robe. When she asked Brendan straight out if he were seeing someone else, he denied it. "For me—and ideally for everyone—there are three genders: Me, the woman I'm seeing, and everybody else. You don't need to be insecure, Joyce. Of all the women I've dated, you're the only one I haven't broken up with yet."

* * *

They finished the last of the appetizers as Joyce completed her story. "That was not much of a denial, when you think about it."

"Yes, but any kind of denial was a lie." Rose was grim. "Did you see him again?"

"Not for a while. His evasions disgusted me. He sent emails I didn't open. He sent flowers. I told my husband to take them to his girlfriend."

"Ouch," said Maxine. "So your husband was still getting lucky."

"Yes, and I wasn't. There are bigger losers than Brendan out there. Trust me, I found them. I took Gary's advice and went on some dates. It's nothing like our college years out there."

* * *

I t had been months since Joyce opened her dating profile. When she did, there were twenty messages. She blocked the senders of gross propositions and deleted the canned "Hello there!" messages. That left three that were marginal possibilities.

S he met Harry at a brightly lit burger place on a big thoroughfare near the bay. His hair looked newly dyed, a flashy sort of black that had never been anyone's real color. He ate his fries in total silence and then said, "OK. I'm done with my coffee. Wanna screw?"

Joyce left five dollars on the table for her coffee, got up and walked out.

* * *

A t a Greek cafe near the base of the Berkeley hills, Joyce ate dinner with Jim, who looked almost too academic in a tweed jacket with suede patches. Something about him actually got her hopes up, until the bill arrived and he took a slim volume from his valise.

"I've so enjoyed meeting you, Joyce. Regrettably, I don't have the funds to pay my portion of dinner. But I can offer you my latest book of poetry, in exchange for my share of the tab."

Joyce stood and picked up the bill. "Keep the book."

* * *

I n a wonderfully kitschy Tiki bar on the bay island of Alameda, Joyce's next date, Barry, proffered a metal and crystal contraption over Mai Tais. "Carry this sacred apparatus with you wherever you go." Barry's voice was sonorous. "Its vibrations will protect you from all bad intent. I'll only charge you for time and materials."

Joyce grabbed her purse and paid for her own drink on the way out.

* * *

Maxine could not help but laugh. "I'm sorry, Joyce. How awful. But so funny!"

Rose shook her head. "Three of them in a row!"

Joyce laughed too. "I know. It's funny to look back on them now. It wasn't funny then. I started telling myself that at this age my expectations were too high."

"Oh no you don't." Maxine was adamant. "That is so wrong."

"After those really crappy first dates I circled back to Brendan. Better the devil you know than the devil you don't, or so I thought. But this time my bullshit detector was on high alert."

* * *

In bed one night, after coldhearted lovemaking when Brendan paid almost clinical attention to her responses, he said to Joyce, "I love talking with you about chemistry. Not to mention *our* chemistry. If we were younger, we'd be planning to have a baby."

"I doubt that. My husband would not approve." And neither would she.

"It's hard for me to picture you with another man."

Joyce had to laugh. "It's not hard for me to picture you with another woman. You get a lot of phone calls while I'm here."

"I do see other women, but only as platonic friends."

"What I'm asking is whether you tell these other women the truth."

"The truth?" Brendan sounded quizzical. "Think about what

happens as we age, and there are more women left than men. Realistically, what should women do about that?"

"How slimy. What are you saying men should do? Lie incessantly?"

"Nothing so crass as that. Really, Joyce, you do have a flair for the dramatic. Unusual for a chemist, but all too common in women."

That Saturday Joyce and Gary drove to North Berkeley and climbed Indian Rock, a boulder the size of a three-story house with steps carved into the granite. From their perch at the top, the entire Bay Area was arrayed before them.

Gary knew that Brendan's attitude and his evasions were grating on Joyce. "I'm sorry I suggested you meet him. You should stop seeing him. For good. Should we go back to being exclusive?"

"No." Joyce stared across the water at the San Francisco skyline. "Polyamory suits you. And what's happening with me isn't Pam's fault."

"If Brendan is lying to women, what he's doing is nothing like polyamory. "

"It is *something* like polyamory. You and he both get laid a lot."

"I know you're hurting. You'll feel better about all this when you meet the right other guy."

* * *

Joyce drank the last of her wine. "And that's when I told Brendan we needed to have a serious talk. And that's when he sent me that ridiculous Pablo Neruda email. And then I heard from Rose. And here we are."

"How messed up is that." Rose shook her head.

Maxine chimed in. "He's revolting."

Rose made up a pseudo-advertising jingle to lighten the mood. "Women in your sixties: Is polyamory right for you?"

Maxine had her own version. "Women in your sixties: Are men right for you?"

"It does make you wonder," said Rose.

"Yes, it does." Joyce shook off her memories. "So, Maxine, now it's your turn: How did you meet Brendan?"

Maxine looked at her watch. "Hey, it's getting late..."

"Oh no, you won't get off that easy," said Joyce. "We spilled our guts. Your turn."

[9]

MAXINE'S TALE

The city of Piedmont is a lagoon of white faces in a rainbow sea. About two square miles of prime real estate is surrounded on all sides by the city of Oakland. Piedmont is what some call a "donut hole," a rich enclave in an urban area. It was once known as the "city of millionaires," with more millionaires per square mile than any city in America.

Back in the early 1900s, when Oakland was a small ambitious town intent on annexing neighboring townships, Piedmont was high on the list. In those days, Piedmont was a mix of rich San Francisco earthquake refugees and bohemians like Jack London. When it came time for Piedmont residents to vote on becoming a separate city, the wealthier residents barely prevailed, by a difference of just eighteen votes. Town leaders worked late nights to draw up and submit incorporation plans. They were in such a rush not to be part of Oakland that they based the city borders on sewage maps. Even today, the edges of the city of Piedmont run right through many people's houses. Oakland's vote to annex Piedmont went forward later that year, and that time, a majority of Piedmont voters chose to join the larger town. But it was too late: Piedmont was already incorporated, and disincorporation required a two-thirds vote that never happened.

These days Piedmont has license plate scanners at every point of entry. It offers nothing to attract Oakland residents—no libraries, no shopping district. The city baseball field has high fences and a locked gate.

In addition to its stately homes, the main attraction for residents is the town's first-class public schools. A hundred years after incorporation, the Piedmont schools have become a "parasite district," a school district funded by the high property taxes on its mansions. In the 1990s a teacher in the Oakland schools photographed the facilities at Oakland High School and at Piedmont High, which are less than two miles apart. She captured the crumbling labs, classrooms and football field at O-High, and pristine, state of the art facilities in Piedmont. She created a slide show that began with the contrasting views of these two schools. Then for comparison she showed photographs of black versus white schools submitted as evidence against the claim of "separate but equal" in the 1954 Supreme Court case, *Brown vs. Board of Education*. Even without overt segregation, the level of separate and unequal was no less stark for the Piedmont and Oakland schools.

When white Berkeley parents stress about moving to Piedmont for the schools, they agonize about their liberal guilt. When Maxine Vargas and her then-husband Charles bought their Piedmont home in the 1980s, they agonized about their children's safety. They knew their real estate dollars would buy access to a first-rate education, but they also knew the tensions their African American children would face in the Piedmont Schools. Tyler was ten when they bought the house and Octavia was seven. On the day they moved in, Maxine went next door to ask to use the phone (this was before cell phones, and the installer had not arrived). The curtain on a window by her neighbor's door fluttered and Maxine could hear a boy about Tyler's age scream out, "Mom! There's a black person at the door!" Not exactly a plate of warm cookies for the new neighbors.

Maxine had just been made a partner at the patent law firm of Stilton Ramsey, and Charles was an Assistant District Attorney for Alameda County. Both had grown up in multiracial families, but it was the black side of their family trees that their neighbors saw. When Charles was pulled over three times in one month within blocks of his own home, he began an investigation of bias in Piedmont traffic stops. The police stopped pulling Charles over, but his boss let him know it would be better for Charles' career if he called off the investigation. That was when Charles began to answer recruiting calls from the Los Angeles District Attorney's Office. A year later Charles was gone, to a better job, a more supportive boss, a new home in Beverly Hills, and a new wife.

Maxine doubled down on her work and her parenting, and the years flew by—lots of years. The children grew up, went to college, moved out. The pandemic hit and Tyler moved back home to his mother's pool house. The pandemic ended and Tyler bought his own home. Suddenly Maxine was in her sixties, no longer a fixture at PTA meetings where for many years she had been the only person of color in the room. Suddenly retirement was not just a distant idea. She could do it if she wanted to. She could walk away from her firm, from the long hours and the office politics. From her preening white male partners. From the internship program she had built to support inventors of color. And then what would she do?

It was a beautiful East Bay Saturday, one of those balmy blue-sky days in July when California seems just a step away from heaven. Maxine and her best friend Gloria relaxed on chaise lounges by Maxine's pool. Until recent years, the two women had been the only African American partners at their law firm, Gloria in patent litigation and Maxine in the group that drafted original patents. Gloria was a short round woman with close-cropped grey hair and an air of barely contained energy.

"We need to lighten up," said Gloria. "It's about time. How many dates have you had in the last year?"

Maxine shook her head.

"OK, the last five years. No? What are we doing with our lives?"

"Gloria, how are we going to meet anybody? Sure, I meet people at work, colleagues and clients, but I can't get involved. You can't either. Or do you?"

"No, not there. I would never date anyone from work."

"Are you dating someone right now?"

"Not really. Once in a while."

"So, this is a case of, 'Do as I say, not as I do.'"

Gloria laughed. "Yes, I admit that. And I love my work. I know you love it too. But one of these days we are going to be old—I mean really old—and what will we do with ourselves?"

"They say nobody on their deathbed regrets not working more. But maybe those people had boring jobs."

Gloria stood up. "Come on."

"Where?"

"We're going to your study. We are going to set up dating profiles online."

"You go ahead."

"You too!"

"No thanks." Maxine folded her arms.

"Let's go. No excuses." Gloria could tell Maxine was about to object. "This is how people meet each other now. Give it a shot."

They took a bottle of tequila and two glasses up to Maxine's study, with its beautifully bound books and antique surveying instruments. On Maxine's desk was a gold framed photograph of her deceased parents, Maria and Eli, when they were in their eighties.

Maxine turned on the computer. "If we were to do this—and I mean *if*—where would we start?"

"With tequila." After two shots Gloria and Maxine were writing outrageous things about themselves. How beautiful they were, how successful, how charming. But their bragging did not begin to match the hot air from one guy.

"Check out this profile," said Gloria. "You have to hand it to a man with this kind of nerve." She read it out loud, punctuated by laughter from Maxine.

We could begin our enchanted evening with chilled champagne, a handful of radishes in fermented butter, and heirloom tomatoes with basil fresh from my window garden. We could then transition to pan roasted wild salmon, paired with organic golden quinoa and grilled broccolini, and an ecstatic Fumé Blanc.

"No way," said Maxine.

"Oh yes, way. But wait, there's more."

We might end the evening with delicately slivered almonds atop organic blueberries marinated in Grand Marnier. A diminutive glass of port could fuel the next phase of our moonlit adventure.

"He sounds like a restaurant ad."

"I dare you, Max. Go on one date with this guy, and I'll take you out to dinner at Chez Panisse."

"Now you're playing hardball. Alright. It's a deal."

* * *

Rose was baffled. "Wait a minute. Why didn't Gloria just go out with Brendan herself?"

"He has the wrong plumbing," said Maxine.

"What do you mean?"

"I mean, Gloria prefers the ladies."

"Ah!" The light went on for Joyce. "So how did it go with you and Brendan?"

Maxine thought back to that first date. "At first it was fine. He was easy to talk with."

* * *

Brendan and Maxine finished dinner at a cozy Italian place in central Berkeley and chatted over coffee.

"...So when I told Charles I was taking back my maiden name, he insisted our divorce agreement stipulate the children would keep his last name. I said that was fine, as long as they kept my mitochondria."

Brendan laughed. "That's marvelous. But he's a district attorney? I doubt he got the joke—unless you explained how it happens that women control a 51% share of the genetic inheritance." He took her hand. "You know, Maxine, I've never met anyone like you."

Maxine smiled. "Nor will you. There is no one like me."

"Brava! Too many women our age are unsure of themselves. They listen to all those negative messages in the culture."

"Well, I don't believe in all that." Maxine looked Brendan right in the eye. "I'm what you might call a Queen Bee. That means any man I date sees only me. No one else."

"Understood. If I were lucky enough to be that guy, no other woman would even cross my mind."

* * *

They went on several dates before Maxine accepted an invitation to dinner at his home.

"Let me show you my humble abode," Brendan said with a flourish. "Here is my simple kitchen, where I will prepare this evening's culinary pleasures." He escorted her around the small house. "My computer station for affairs of the mind, and my bedroom for affairs of the heart."

On his bed was a comforter appliquéd with a single large Chinese character.

"What does this symbol mean?" Maxine brushed the fabric lightly.

"It's the ideogram for poetry," said Brendan. "Beautiful, isn't it?

And it suits us so well, my dear, since we both love the language. I admire your mind, the way you understand science as well as words. All true geniuses are polymaths. Why haven't people like us just set up a colony at the North Pole and taken over?" He sat on the bed and patted the place next to him. "Here, come sit with me."

The problem was, Brendan was so outrageous he was irresistible. The bombast. The unabashed narcissism. In bed one night after they made love, Brendan actually said to her, "I don't need to stand on the shoulders of giants. I just stand on tiptoe." Maxine laughed when she repeated that to Gloria.

Her friend shook her head. "You find that ego appealing, don't you?"

"I do. Brendan makes me laugh."

Plus, he was a really good lover. He listened with a practiced ear to her sounds in ecstasy. He must have had some sorting device in his brain where he stored the memories of what turned on every woman he had been with. "You are one of those women who could come just from someone caressing your back," he said to her one night with admiration. She felt she had joined an elite category that by his age might include hundreds. From his tales of exploits past, it was clear she was far from the only woman with a soft spot for narcissists.

Brendan loved talking about science. Every patent lawyer must have a degree in science, and Maxine's bachelors degree was in engineering. Brendan asked her oddly specific questions, like, "Tell me: what are the constraints on materials for solar panels?" And, "What are the capacity limits on downloading current from solar rooftops?"

He also loved talking about the law, especially patent law. Out of curiosity, Maxine looked him up on the Patent Office database and found that Brendan Burns did not hold a single patent, even though he talked a good game.

One night when they were naked in bed he said, "The law on patenting genetic sequences has really changed in the last ten years."

Maxine, who really did love her field, said, "That is true, it's much more restrictive. Back in the eighties, companies were able to patent naturally occurring genomes. Not anymore."

"But if you improve on a naturally occurring process, like, say, photosynthesis, that's different, isn't it?"

"Sure, biomimetics can be patented. The interesting thing is what happens at the margins. When is it just enough of a change to justify a patent? Hence the lucrative careers of my partners in litigation."

"I so enjoy talking with you, Maxine. You have no idea how close we are."

"You're a lucky guy, Brendan Burns."

"You're lucky too, Maxine. A lot of men my age have passed their sell-by dates."

They saw each other a few times a week for a couple months. It was not exactly a romance, but it would do for now. Then one morning when Maxine left Brendan's house to go to work, somebody had sprayed shaving cream all over her new Audi. She walked around her sedan, incredulous. It was covered in suds. There was white stuff everywhere, fluffy, like frosting.

Maxine knocked on Brendan's door and then walked in.

"Brendan," she said, "somebody's vandalized my car. It seems to have white paint all over it."

Brendan was seated at his computer, typing. "Oh really?" He did not look up.

"Yes, really! Do you know why someone would do that?"

"No."

"I need to get to the office."

"Oh."

His lack of reaction was bizarre.

"Where do you keep a bucket and a sponge?"

"You might find what you need in the hall closet."

Maxine used the bucket of water and the sponge to remove as much of the foam as she could without ruining her dress clothes.

Brendan gave no apology, voiced no concern, never offered to help. Never even looked up from his computer. Some of the inventors Maxine worked with had atypical social skills, and Maxine knew she was not exactly a diplomat herself. But the way he reacted that day was so odd, almost like he expected it to happen.

* * *

Maxine gave her companions a knowing look. "So, which of you did it?"

Joyce frowned. "Did what?"

"Which of you sprayed my car that night?"

"Wasn't me," said Rose.

"Not me either," said Joyce.

"Really?"

Joyce and Rose shook their heads.

"OK maybe." Maxine sounded skeptical. "If you say so. But then who was it?"

"There was nobody else in Brendan's 'Personal' email folder," said Rose. "Only the three of us. It's a mystery."

* * *

And then—to top it off—Brendan left a message saying he was having minor surgery and would stay at a friend's house the entire next week.

Maxine told Gloria, who wasn't buying it. "Come on, Max, you don't believe this guy, do you?"

"He claims he's only seeing me. That's our agreement."

"Yeah, but think about that crazy business with the shaving cream."

"Maybe that was a random act of vandalism."

Gloria scoffed. "Maybe the Easter Bunny is real. Tell you what: Let's go see if he's really staying with a friend, or if he's home tonight."

Maxine put her hands on her hips. "I will not stoop to spying on someone I'm dating."

"OK, then I'll go by myself," said Gloria.

"Alright. I can't stop you. But call me if you see anything."

"I won't be able to resist."

That night after work, Gloria drove her Porsche to Brendan's street. A beat-up Mercedes was parked outside his home. All his lights were on.

"Alright you bastard," she whispered. "Got you."

Gloria parked and walked across the yard. She looked through Brendan's living room window and saw a big white man watching television. He had his arm around someone. The figure was indistinct, but clearly a woman, sitting beside him on the couch. Gloria took a photo and texted it to Maxine.

Maxine called Brendan on his cell. When Brendan's phone rang, Gloria watched Brendan rise and walk away from his guest to answer it.

"Hello Brendan," said Maxine.

"Yes? Hi Maxine."

"How are you feeling?"

"Starting to feel better. Glad I'm over at my friend's house so they can take care of me."

"Does your friend live at your place?"

"Whatever do you mean?"

"You were sitting on your couch just now. At home. And you have company." Maxine hung up the phone. Brendan stared at his phone for a moment, then looked up at the window where Gloria stood.

Gloria had seen enough and walked back to her car.

* * *

By now, the after-work crowd at The Lab had finished their drinks and gone home. With sidelong glances at the three women sitting at the corner table, the waitstaff began to wipe down tables.

"And that night, ladies, is when I sent Brendan the email saying we should talk. I'm not sure why I bothered. And what he wrote back was so insulting—well, we have all seen that ludicrous Pablo Neruda email."

Joyce snorted. "The man is a complete asshat. I don't know whether to pee or vomit."

"Maybe both," said Rose. "Shall we adjourn to the facilities?"

All three women rose, a bit wobbly from drink, and headed for the Ladies Room. Consistent with the theme of The Lab, the walls were adorned with double helix wallpaper. All three stalls were occupied. Joyce, Maxine, and Rose waited in line, trying to stand steady.

Rose held a sink for balance and tried to make conversation. "I read a study where they swabbed the toilet seats in public bathrooms. Turns out the farthest stall from the door has the lowest bacterial load."

"Really?" Joyce demurred. "The study I read showed definitively that the middle stall has the lowest count."

The toilet in the nearest stall flushed. Maxine was on it. "That's great news, but somebody is leaving the first stall and I don't care how many bacteria it has, so if you ladies will just step aside—"

As a woman exited the nearest stall, Joyce, Rose and Maxine all lunged for it.

"That is my toilet. I was here first," said Joyce.

"I need to go the worst," said Rose.

Maxine shook her head. "That makes no sense, Rose—how would you know that?"

Rose was slightly dizzy. She wondered what she had been thinking, to suggest meeting these two women. It would not get Brendan back. It would not put things back to the way they had been when she first met him. Hardly aware that she was speaking out loud, she said, "I wish I'd never written to either of you."

"Oh yeah?" Joyce was an angry drunk.

"Hey—we all got played. No need to take it out on each other. Let's take it out on him." Maxine was all logic, alcohol or not.

Two women left the middle and far stalls. Maxine took the first stall, Joyce took the middle stall, and Rose took the far stall. All three doors slammed in a most satisfying manner.

* * *

Maxine had not taken a sick day in years, but the headache that woke her the next morning left no choice. She emailed her assistant letting her know she was out ill and to please reschedule her meetings. Then she took a headache pill and found a nice dark room where she could sit on a lounge chair with an icebag on her head.

What a night. That Rose was an odd bird, reaching out and then getting all huffy about it. But what a situation. Her friend Gloria had been right all along about Brendan, and Maxine had been too stubborn to see it.

At ten in the morning she took a call from Gloria.

"Hello?"

"Hi. You sound horrible."

"I feel horrible."

"What is it? The flu?"

"Hangover."

Gloria laughed. "You're kidding, right? Since when do you drink enough to get hung over?"

"When I meet the two other women my monogamous manfriend is dating."

"No! That jackass is no damn good."

"How true. The three of us got drunk at a bar last night and traded stories."

"Oh, that is rich. I want to hear all about it. But how did you leave things? Are you going to meet those women again?"

"I don't know. It ended strangely. The woman who blew the whistle on him got ticked off at the end."

"It's a weird situation, isn't it? Maybe she hoped it was all a mistake."

"Maybe. Anyway I'm glad she told us, and I'm done with that jerk, obviously. I hope the others are too."

"You could write to them. Thank them for their honesty, let them know your breakup plans, 'hope you kick his sorry ass too,' etcetera."

"Yeah, alright. I will. Once this headache is gone." Maxine spent the rest of the day dozing in her lounger, musing about her next email to Joyce and Rose.

BREAKUPS AND BACKSLIDING

"What you've got here is some fabulous material." Claudia Chen sat behind the antique oak desk in her home office like an empress on her throne. Her publishing house, Dolphin Press, was headquartered in Berkeley, but post-pandemic Claudia still enjoyed working from her elegant Piedmont house several days a week. She was almost sixty and at the height of her beauty, with long black hair and a generous smile. Across from Claudia sat her neighbor Maxine, who had just given a recap of the three women's tales from The Lab.

Claudia smiled. "I've always admired your bravery, Max, moving into this white enclave, paving the way for more people of color. And now you've got the makings of a brave book."

"What? You must be joking." Maxine shook her head. "I have a job, Claudia. A more-than-full-time job. How would I find time to write such a thing? And anyway, I'm no novelist."

Claudia waved aside Maxine's objections. "Three older women owning their sexuality. Pushing back on invisibility. And a sexy, articulate bad guy. This is great stuff. You may not be a novelist, but you've been a writer your whole career. Branch out! Try something new!"

"Alright, I admit it: I've always had a secret desire to write a novel."

"Aha!" Claudia looked triumphant.

"But is it fiction if it's about something that actually happened?"

Claudia gestured toward the bookcase behind her. "Most of the debut novels my press publishes have characters and plots based on reality. They say to write what you know, and there's nothing wrong with that. Life handed you a unique lemon, so make unique lemonade."

Maxine laughed. "It does sound fun."

Claudia wagged her finger. "Ah, but what's the next chapter of your story?"

"Maybe we won't know until it happens."

"Fair enough. I know you, Maxine. You're made of strong stuff and if you commit to write this you'll follow through. I'm ready to sign a contract with you, based on the premise alone. And I'm prepared to offer a healthy advance. Don't disappoint me."

"Thank you, Claudia. Maybe it is time to write something other than patents." Maxine reached across the desk and shook Claudia's hand. "It's a great idea. You'll be glad you did this."

* * *

Maxine's email calling for a general strike against Brendan met a receptive audience.

"I'm ready to give him the boot," Joyce emailed back.

"So am I," wrote Rose.

"I'd love to go first," Maxine asked.

"Be our guest," said Rose.

"Copy that," said Joyce.

"Thanks," said Maxine. "I'll let you know how it goes."

* * *

On Solano Avenue at the swank Northern edge of Berkeley is a French Bistro with a dark wooden bar, cozy tables and blue café curtains. The week after Maxine met Rose and Joyce, she sat at a corner table eating French onion soup. Across the table Brendan was having the same. The spoon was small in his hand as he lifted the broth to his fleshy lips.

Maxine looked at him appraisingly. "You and I have never discussed my interest in writing."

Brendan kept eating. "Really? I know you write patents for a living."

"As a partner in my firm, I mentor more than write. But in any case, writing patents isn't the same as writing for enjoyment."

"No, I suppose not. But how would you find the time?"

Maxine tore a corner of baguette from the basket between them. "I'm cutting back my hours at the firm. I am retirement age, after all. And it's amazing what you can fit in, when you're motivated. I've had this idea for a novel."

"Oh? What is it?" Brendan glanced around the room. He seemed more interested in the other diners than in what Maxine was saying.

She carried on, undeterred. "The book is about three smart women in their sixties. One is a chemist, one a biologist, and one is a patent lawyer. They find out they are all dating the same man, but he's telling each of them he is only seeing her."

Now Brendan looked at her. He set down his spoon. "Ah."

Maxine continued. "And he questions each of them about photosynthesis, of all things. I haven't worked that out yet—why this character talks with all three women about that particular reaction. But it's early days."

Brendan lifted his wineglass. "Yes. Well, as you know I subscribe to multiverse theory. Everything that can happen, does. There is at least one universe where your character is faithful to each of these women."

Maxine laughed. "That assumes there are at least three universes in which this character is not a jackass."

Brendan sat up straight and assumed a dignified mien. "If men realized that honesty was an option, they would use it. They feel they must lie to get laid. I choose to think that they are victims."

Maxine smiled. "How creative."

"I can see that trust has been broken. Perhaps we should end this." He continued his attempt to look dignified.

Maxine was not impressed. "Oh, trust me, we *have* ended this. My only regret is that you are such a great source of material. My publisher will be sorry. I signed a contract with her today. The book will be called *Brilliant Charming Bastard*, although the "Brilliant" part may be a stretch. This dinner is my treat, by the way; we're celebrating my advance."

"Mazel tov. I think."

"Thank you." Maxine raised her glass of red wine.

Brendan did not raise his glass in return. "But if you're writing about me, you're carrying a torch."

"Not at all." Maxine took a sip of her wine. "Writing about an ex isn't carrying a torch. It's carrying a blowtorch."

Brendan's face turned red. "You're not the only three women in the world. You're not special. Not one of you."

"And that, you sad buffoon, is exactly where you are wrong."

The waiter brought their main course to the table. Brendan looked up. "Could you box mine, please? I find I have no appetite."

"Of course, Sir. And for you, Madam?"

"Thank you, Louis. I will enjoy mine right here."

And after that, she thought, *I'll write my new friends about this little* tête-à-tête.

* * *

J oyce knew that Maxine was right: The time had come to end things with Brendan for good. It was impossible to make him mend his ways; the best she could hope for was to speak her piece.

The following Tuesday, Joyce sat at the sushi bar in a Japanese restaurant just downhill from Indian Rock, staring at her untouched dragon roll. Brendan was next to her, thoroughly enjoying his shrimp nigiri.

Joyce glared as she turned to face him. "I told you over and over that I expected honesty."

Brendan licked unagi sauce from his fingers. "Yes, you did tell me that. Over and over, as you say. I just read a study that showed nagging is the leading cause of divorce, ahead of infidelity. Something to think about." He picked up a piece of sushi and dipped it in sauce. "Your problem, Joyce, is that you won't take yes for an answer. I was giving you everything you could reasonably expect. And more."

Joyce tuned him out, looking straight ahead. "I need to live my life with integrity. And I expect integrity from the people close to me. Navigating an open marriage is a challenge. It requires consideration, and scrupulous honesty."

Brendan shook his head. "Love is more like reading a novel: We must suspend our disbelief. That kind of credulity is essential to how you deal with me, and with your husband."

"You're talking about fiction. I'm talking about life."

Brendan put down his chopsticks. "Everything we do is fiction. The world we see is just a model, it's not objective reality. The way you present yourself is fiction. Look at you: You look like a church lady and fuck like a rabbit."

Joyce ignored the sniggers from the sushi chef behind the bar. "You used to tell me that when you're with a woman, it's as if nobody else is female. You knew I was polyamorous. You didn't need to say such things. What were you doing? Keeping your lies consistent?"

Brendan gestured, his stubby fingers in the air. "This cloud of women surrounds me. I don't invite them. They just arrive. And yes, I always have a backup plan—and so should you."

Joyce put her head in her hands. "I need to be strong."

Brendan sipped his sake. "Great, be strong. If you want to change, just change. That's what I do."

"That's exactly it: you don't change. You are incapable of change —so this conversation is pointless." Joyce leaned down and picked up her purse. "Goodbye, Brendan."

As Joyce walked out the door, Brendan took a bite of her dragon roll.

* * *

In her moments of clarity, Rose could only thank Joyce and Maxine for paving the way for her goodbye to Brendan. She steeled herself to let him go.

On the island of Alameda, in the San Francisco Bay off the Oakland shore, is a Burmese restaurant famous for its fabulous spicy food. The place scraped by selling takeout at the height of the pandemic, then went right back to being packed every night. But Rose and Brendan were there at five on a Wednesday, and they had some elbow room.

Rose warmed her hands on the cup of tea in front of her.

Brendan was expostulating. "You're taking a position, as if you think it's noble."

"Not at all. This is exactly what I want to do. You know how you always say a man leaves a woman for another woman, and a woman leaves a man for another life."

"Don't quote me at me. I have also told you many times that possessiveness is the opposite of love. I fell in love with you thinking you were capable of loving me."

"I did love you. Or I thought I did. But it made no sense, even before I met Maxine and Joyce. Maybe it was more like obsession."

"All love contains a hint of obsession, don't you think?"

Rose shook her head. "No, I don't believe that."

"Rose, I can tell you are unhappy. In fact, the main difference between us is that I have been happy. You have not. You're simply unable to accept unconditional love."

"Unconditional love?" Rose's voice was rising.

Just then the waiter brought their plates of food. Rose took a deep breath and continued quietly. "Unconditional love? That's what you call lying to three different women?"

Brendan opened his mouth to answer but Rose talked over him. "I hated coming here tonight. But I needed to tell you that what you did was wrong. All that lying. All that pretending. You never understood that I was the most interesting person you knew. And I never, not once, wanted to be on your list of spare parts."

"You're not a spare part. You are my leading lady. The rest are just understudies. I was beautiful once, you know. When I'm with you I feel beautiful again."

"And when I'm with you I feel like a prize fool. We're finished here." Rose stood up.

Brendan picked up the check and held it out to her. "I'm a bit tapped out at the moment, Rose. Could you take care of this?"

Rose paid no heed and walked away.

"It's done," she emailed Joyce and Maxine. "We are three for three."

* * *

But was she done?

A week went by, then two.

I miss him, thought Rose, *I can't help it.*

Despite her brave words to Linda about carrying on with a broken heart, Rose found it difficult to sketch out her upcoming lectures and write her exams. She tried to understand what she was feeling. She remembered exactly what the end was like with Brendan and did not miss that at all. It was the beginning of their affair that called to her.

Rose wanted that again. She wanted to be admired. She wanted to be seduced. And she could have it. She knew how she could.

Rose got online and found a photograph of a dead woman her age. It was appallingly easy; she was now of an age when too many died.

And suddenly, online, Rose became a woman Brendan had never met.

She ignored the requirement to make only one "Unique Profile" on the dating website, and the part about only joining for the purpose of a *bona fide* relationship. She agreed to the very rules she was there to break. Rose was now Kate, the cyberstalker granny.

Rose had read up on dealing with narcissists, and she knew how to beat them at their game: be a bigger narcissist than they were. Tall order, in this case.

But you can't keep him, she told herself. *You can only tempt him. If you keep him, you lose.*

Rose sent Brendan his first message from Kate.

Let me guess.
You are a man who takes prisoners, not lovers.
A relationship with you is like an ill-advised shopping spree:
You rack up a huge balance,
knowing full well you'll be presented with the bill.
Tell me that I'm wrong.

"*Kate,*" he wrote back. "*At last we meet.*"

This business of cyberstalking was not something she wanted to admit to Joyce and Maxine, nor to her daughter. But later that week Rose stopped by Linda and Rick's house and let it slip.

By now Rose had told Linda the stories from The Lab, and it

seemed that Linda had repeated them to Rick. He caught Rose alone in the kitchen. "I assume the Brendan thing is over."

"Almost. I still write to him. Anonymously."

Rick shook his head. "Linda told me you met two women who dated him while you did, and that he lied to all of you. That dude is bad news. Listen, I'm a guy, but I'm not always proud of my gender, especially when I hear about men like that. And it might be worse than you think. For all you know, he could be cooking meth or filming porn in that creepy house of his."

"Aren't you being slightly paranoid?"

"No, I'm not. I've been around people like that. They make you feel like you're crazy. You've got to get rid of him completely. What would you say if your daughter told you I was behaving like Brendan did, telling that woman I was in a different city when I was really at my house?"

"I'd tell her if she stayed with you, she wasn't taking care of herself."

"That's right."

"But I'm not with him—"

"No contact, Rose. None."

When you've been conned, thought Rose, *and you realize it, yet you miss being conned, you've been in the presence of a real artist.*

* * *

It was clear to Maxine that of the three of them, Rose would have the hardest time putting Brendan behind her. When she did not hear from Rose except the tersest of emails, Maxine called Joyce to ask if Rose had reached out to her.

"Not a word."

"I'm going to see if I can visit."

"Seems like a good idea." Joyce sighed. "Rose may actually have loved that bastard."

Maxine called to ask if she could stop by Rose's house one day after work.

"I guess," said Rose. Not much enthusiasm, but neither was it a no. The next day Maxine was sitting in Rose's living room.

"What a charming little bungalow." Maxine took in the Craftsman fireplace and ignored the grime in the corners. "I do love Berkeley. There's nowhere else like it."

"Yeah." Rose sat on the couch in a bathrobe. Her hair looked unwashed.

"How are you, Rose? You seem a bit down."

"I'm alright. I don't know, I just miss that bastard, even knowing everything I know about him."

"OK. I hear that. So, what are you doing to take care of yourself?"

Rose snorted. "Yeah. Take care of myself. Even giving myself the benefit of the doubt, which I don't really deserve, there is no justification for keeping up this charade."

"What charade? What are you talking about?"

"It's easy to push his little buttons. Of course, he is predictable and automatic. Of course, he can be played. I've proven it. I don't need to keep proving it."

"Rose, what on earth—"

"The one thing I wanted to say to him, I've already said: He had no idea that I was the most interesting person he knew. No offense, Maxine. And now I need to be the most interesting person I know."

"What the devil are you playing at, Rose?"

"I cannot reveal myself to him by voice or in person, so I have to shut it down. Good riddance. Being a cyberstalker is a bad idea on so many levels that I can't even list them."

"Oh." Maxine began to understand. "You've been in touch with him. Under an alias, I hope."

"Yes. I have."

"We both know who he is. A guy like that doesn't let go easily. He just keeps finding ways to degrade you. No matter who you are, no matter what you look like, no matter how wonderful you may be. Real self, fake self, doesn't matter."

"I am infested," said Rose. "Like a mouse with toxoplasmosis in love with a cat. I carry him in my brain."

"No, you're not infested. You're an intelligent woman. Listen." Maxine leaned in toward Rose. "Make a list of what was wrong and carry it with you. If you're tempted to contact him, take the list out and read it. Leave Brendan alone and live your life. It's important to trust ourselves, but it's also important to recognize when we can't trust ourselves, when we need to consult other people. Talk with Joyce. Talk with me. We'll give you a reality check."

"OK." Rose still sounded flat.

"Plus, half the people in the East Bay are therapists. Make an appointment with one, if you think it would help. Be nice to yourself in ways that make sense. Not eating-a-gallon-of-ice-cream nice. And not by writing to that bastard. Pay attention to yourself and what really serves you. Take a hike. Go to the beach." Maxine looked around. "And I'll send over my housekeeper to do a deep clean. Just a little thank-you gift from me to you."

"Why are you helping me?"

"Because you told me the truth. And truth is the highest good. And because we have a lot to do, you and me and Joyce."

"Do? About what?"

"Go take a shower. Get yourself right. And one day soon, when you're ready, the three of us will talk."

* * *

In a fine old neighborhood on the island of Alameda, there is a restored Victorian house converted to therapy offices. Surrounded by ancient oaks, it sits among grand homes with only a discreet sign on the veranda to distinguish it from its neighbors. Rose walked into the lobby and climbed wood paneled stairs to the top floor, where she sat in the waiting room.

Stephanie opened her office door. She was a full-bodied woman in her forties with close-cropped hair. "Welcome, Rose. Please, come in, sit. How are you?"

How was she? Rose could still see Brendan in her mind's eye, the real Brendan, the man he was meant to be. That man suited her entirely. But every time she had tried to reach that man it was as if plate glass was in the way and she became a bird, throwing herself against the glass, certain that despite the pain there was nothing in the way. That was how she was.

"I understand," said Stephanie. "It's painful to look back when we've ignored our instincts, when we knew a relationship was bad for us. It's tough to see that we have put someone else at the center of our lives and not taken care of ourselves. How often were you told as a little girl to be quiet and pleasing? How often was your assertiveness labeled as bossiness? We are taught we must betray ourselves or be alone. It's a devil's bargain, and we must break it."

When Rose stopped and stood back, she saw what a fool she had forced herself to be. When she stopped, it was a different neighborhood of self, a more spacious place. From that day on, Rose danced and swam every day. It was liberating to be freed from Brendan's couch, where she had spent many a weekend, sharing his torpor. It was liberating to have her own thoughts.

* * *

A week later, Brendan drove to Piedmont and knocked on Maxine's front door with an edible fruit bouquet in his hands. Pineapple spears mixed with kiwi and citrus—it was quite sprightly and, he thought, eminently appealing.

Maxine opened the door, saw who it was, and slammed the door shut.

He drove up San Pablo Avenue to Joyce's house and knocked on the door, holding the same fruit bouquet. Joyce looked through the peephole, saw Brendan, and sent her husband to answer the door.

"Leave now or I'll call the police." Gary towered over the man on his porch. "Don't come back here. Ever."

Brendan spun around briskly. He drove back down to Berkeley, to Rose's house, and knocked on her door with the bouquet, now slightly ragged, in his hands.

Rose opened the door. There he was again, all white hair and bouquet. As if a bunch of fruit would make up for all the lying. As if he could pull that stunt one more time and weasel his way back into her good graces and her bed. A bouquet in his hands and mischief in his heart. No apology of course. That was not his style. Or more accurately, his *modus operandi*. 'Style' was too benign a term for this lying misogynistic narcissistic rascal. She remembered the first time he brought her a bouquet of flowers, before she was onto him. It worked like a charm back then. The promise of long slow kisses and lazy afternoons in bed mesmerized her. He was so knowing, she remembered. So practiced a lover.

"Aren't you going to invite me in?" He smiled. "And by 'in,' I don't necessarily mean 'in.'"

That stale joke again. The fruit in his hand trembled with suppressed laughter. Her therapist was right: It was time to delete the Kate profile, finally, right now. Rose slammed the door and went to her computer.

Brendan shrugged and walked away, nibbling a drooping spear of pineapple. On to the next adventure.

[11]
A NEW ERA

axine met Rose at her house and they walked up the street to the Sconehenge Café. Aromas of coffee and waffles drifted from tables full of talkative Berkeley denizens. The plate glass window gave them a cattycorner view of the Berkeley Bowl, an organic grocer that got its start in a long-ago bowling alley. A quizzical Joyce arrived and slid into their booth. "Well, Maxine? What's this about?"

"Thanks for coming, Joyce. You too, Rose. I wanted to let you know that I've signed a contract with an old friend who runs a publishing house. The working title for my novel is *Brilliant Charming Bastard*. It's about three women scientists who discover they are dating the same lying dilettante."

Joyce laughed. "Why does that sound familiar?"

Rose looked serious. "Congratulations, Maxine. More power to you. But why tell us?"

"Because I believe there is more to this story than we've talked about. Remember how Brendan kept quizzing the two of you about photosynthesis?"

Rose looked down at folded hands. "I'd rather move on from talking about Brendan."

"Understood. But give me a little latitude. This may be important."

"Alright," said Joyce. "We're listening."

Maxine nodded. "At the same time he was talking botany with you, he was grilling me about patent law. Not about biotechnology, which I wouldn't have known about anyway, but about engineering issues, especially solar panels."

Joyce threw up her hands. "So what? As you said, the man is a dilettante."

"Agreed. But maybe he had a purpose."

"OK, I'll bite," said Joyce. "All that stuff about the chemistry of photosynthesis. How it could be improved."

"Yes, and solar panels. What they're made from and why." Maxine leaned forward. "Just think: What if Brendan wasn't just using us for sex? What if he was using our minds?"

Rose frowned. "What do you mean?"

"What if we were his involuntary consultants?"

"Sure. Why not exploit our brains too?" Joyce snorted. "I wouldn't put it past him. But what was he up to? What was this big invention that never happened?"

Rose waved her hands. "Wait. Check this out. I just read an article about a new regulation in Paris: If you want to install a roof, it has to either generate solar power or be a garden."

Their mimosas arrived. Maxine traced a line in the condensation on her glass. "And?"

Rose nodded. "What if one roof could do both?"

"You mean, half solar panels and half plants?" Joyce took a sip.

Rose put on her best professor voice. "No. What if you had roof panels with microscopic bioengineered plants that did two jobs: First, break down carbon dioxide to generate oxygen, but a lot more efficiently than natural plants. And second, what if they also created electricity? So the roof would clean the air and provide sustainable energy."

"You think Brendan was trying to invent that?" Maxine was excited now.

"Remember how keen he was on biomimetics? He was always talking about borrowing ideas from nature." Rose sat back as their food arrived.

Joyce laughed. "Yeah. Big on borrowed ideas, isn't he?"

"Seems like it. And whatever he was working on, he planned to patent it. You know he needs money, driving around that beater Mercedes."

"He needed our help to invent this thing. But what do you bet he was going to take all the credit? No wonder he showed up with that rotten fruit bouquet. He was fresh out of ideas." Joyce looked at her companions. "And as long as we three didn't know each other, we couldn't collaborate."

"But now we can. I spent that year with Brendan studying the biological research on modified photosynthesis," said Rose.

Joyce nodded. "And I was studying the chemistry of the reaction."

"Alright." Maxine folded her arms. "I admit I did some reading on solar energy. So if that's what he was doing, that goes in my book. But what then? What's the next chapter?"

Joyce looked thoughtful. "We could beat him to the punch. I've been with Sirona Pharmaceuticals for decades. I've done very well by them. Maybe it's time to work for myself."

"I already work for myself," said Maxine. "I'm a partner at my firm."

Rose asked her, "How would you like to be president of a startup instead?"

"You and I would run the labs, Rose," said Joyce.

"Yes, absolutely. I can retire from teaching when the term ends, and I'd love to take a chance on this."

Maxine nodded. "I hear that. I'm ready for something new."

"I like it." Joyce raised her glass. "No rocking chairs for us, ladies."

Rose clinked glasses. "Are we really doing this? You know the devil is in the details."

Maxine clinked too. "Get thee behind me, Satan. Truth really is stranger than fiction."

* * *

Two weeks later Rose turned sixty-five. Maxine showed up with a cake, and Joyce brought wine and ice cream. The three of them sat in Rose's kitchen. "Thanks, ladies." Rose took a bite of frosting. "Whipped chocolate. My favorite."

"Being in our sixties is more fun than I expected," said Maxine.

"True." Rose took a sip of wine. "We have the means to retire. That's the good news. But if we're serious about starting a company, where would we get the cash?"

"Well..." Maxine looked unsure.

The wheels were spinning for Joyce. "There's a lab building where I work that is scheduled to be torn down and replaced next year. They've already moved everybody into newer digs. I bet Facilities would give us a deal on a one-year lease. They weren't expecting to make a dime. It's pretty run down, and some people say it's haunted."

"Joyce, that's great." Maxine paused. "We need ready money though."

"One thing at a time, Maxine." Rose scooped ice cream onto their cake plates.

"If I'm going to run this thing, I say we tackle it all at once." Maxine looked around the kitchen. "Hey, Rose, what do you owe on your place?"

Rose looked startled. "What, this little bungalow? I just paid it off. I bought it thirty years ago, when I became a professor. But, you know, I live here."

"You should come see the guest house behind my place," Maxine said. "It's bigger than your house."

"That's very kind of you Maxine, but how would that help? This tiny place can't be worth much."

"Oh yeah? Let's look it up. Just to see." Joyce pulled out her phone. "Tell me the street number again."

Rose told her and Joyce showed her an online home value site. Under the picture of Rose's bungalow was a number she could scarcely believe.

"Holy shit! Two million dollars? It cost me fifty thousand, back in the day."

"This is California, man." Joyce zipped her phone back into her bag. "And it's Berkeley."

Maxine drummed her fingers. "Two million would buy a lot of labware."

"Damn yeah," said Joyce. "Rose, just imagine. But if we really did it, what would we call this venture of ours?"

Rose looked thoughtful. "How about Canopy? Like the canopy of a forest, where the trees meet the sun and the magic happens."

"Canopy Enterprises," said Maxine.

"Canopy," said Joyce. "I like it."

Rose raised her glass. "Ladies, a toast: To doing well by doing good."

"Indeed," said Maxine, "Getting rich is the best revenge."

"Copy that," said Joyce.

* * *

Linda Bingham Jones was worried about her mother. She knew that her mom had finally broken up with that jackass Brendan, but she did not know the circumstances and was not sure what to expect. One thing she never anticipated was a FOR SALE sign on the lawn of her childhood home. She knocked on the door and Rose opened it, all smiles.

"Wait—Mom—you're selling our house?"

Rose took the hand of her only child and led her into the bungalow. "It's *my* house, darling. You have a very nice house in another town."

"That's valid. Let's start over. Wait—Mom—you're selling your house?"

"Yes! You would not believe what this little shack is worth these days."

"How much?"

"Plenty to buy all the lab equipment and supplies for a whole new company."

"What new company?"

"The one I'm starting with my friends, Joyce and Maxine."

"I see." Linda tried to stay calm. "And where will you live?"

"Maxine is deeding me her guest house in Piedmont. She hasn't used it since her son moved out. It's lovely. And bigger than this place."

"How long have you known Maxine?"

"It's been almost two months."

"You're moving in with a woman you just met?"

"That's right."

"Are you lovers?"

"No."

"How do you know these women?"

"We were all dating Brendan. At the same time."

"Oh, it's *those* women!" Linda was sure her head would explode. "And the three of you are doing a startup? Where?"

"In Emeryville. Joyce works for a company that has extra lab space. She's negotiating a no-rent deal as part of her retirement package."

"Have you thought this through? At all? What are you doing for health insurance?"

"This crazy little thing called Medicare. Really, everybody should have it."

"It can't be that simple. There has to be something we're forgetting."

"It will come to you, Linda. You're just having a junior moment."

"Oh Mom."

* * *

I t was a Friday afternoon when Rose finished her last lecture of the week and packed up to walk home. Three weeks to go, in the term and in her teaching career. She would miss the university. She was especially going to miss her students. And at that moment, two of her favorites, Isis and Marisol, climbed the stairs to the lecture platform.

"Dr. Bingham," said Isis. "We wondered if we could talk for a minute."

"Sure." Rose stopped packing and gave them her full attention.

"We went online to register for next semester and couldn't find your name on any of the courses."

"Right. Maybe I should mention to my classes that I'm retiring at the end of the term."

"Dr. Bingham! No! You're not!" Marisol stomped her foot. "I really want you to stay."

"I can't, sorry. I really can't."

"Won't you be bored?"

"Just the opposite. I'm founding a new company with two other women. We'll be so busy our heads will spin."

"Where?"

"Down the hill, in Emeryville."

Isis looked excited. "Are you offering summer internships?"

"I don't know. I'll check. But then, I'm one of the owners, so I could probably say yes."

"Terrific!"

"That's great!" Marisol and Isis high-fived.

"Don't you even want to know what we're doing?"

"Well, yeah," said Isis, "but I'm sure it will be cool."

"It actually is. We are designing a new kind of solar panel that runs on photosynthesis."

"The most important chemical reaction in the world!" Marisol recited.

Rose smiled. "Just so. I wonder where you learned that?"

"Alright, Dr. Bingham," said Isis. "Let's get to the important stuff: How much are you going to pay us?"

"Probably nothing, sorry to say. Even the owners are working for nothing until we get investors."

Isis and Marisol looked at each other and shrugged. "We'll do it anyway," Isis said.

Rose smiled. "That's wonderful of you both. I'll check with my partners, but I'm sure we can welcome you to Canopy."

* * *

California is the land of the all-cash deal, and home sales move quickly. Five weeks later, Rose was directing the movers in her living room full of boxes. When the bungalow was empty, Rose took a fond look at the place she had called home for most of her adult life. She was leaving the house where she had raised her child, the house near the university where she built her career. And she was ready, truly ready. It was time.

By mid-afternoon the movers had unloaded Rose's worldly goods into the well-maintained guest house behind Maxine's Colonial Revival. Rose looked around with satisfaction and then opened a box of fossils.

Maxine knocked at her open door. "Welcome, neighbor. Want a break? Wine and appetizers by the pool?"

In tank tops, shorts and sunglasses, the women reclined on loungers by the blue water. Sangria and nachos were laid out on a table between them.

"This is the life, Maxine. I can't begin to thank you. This place is an oasis. How long have you lived here?"

"I bought it twenty years ago, with my then-husband. In those days Piedmont was pricey but not yet ridiculous. At first, the neighbors had a hard time accepting us. Back then we were the only family of color on the street."

"Oh, Maxine. With all your hard work and success, to think that crap still happens."

"You sound like my mom. She was white, and she thought living in a fancy neighborhood would keep me safe. 'Are you doing alright?' she would ask. 'People being kind to you?'"

"She wouldn't have thought much of how Brendan treated you."

"She wouldn't have thought much of how Brendan treated any of us. But she didn't live to see it. We had her in a great nursing home, but COVID still took her."

"I'm so sorry."

"Yeah. Me too."

"What's it like around here now?"

"It's gotten better. Slowly. We went from being the neighborhood pariahs to the neighborhood trophy ornaments: the black people who prove how tolerant rich white people can be of corporate lawyers. But if somebody they don't know is driving while black in this town, they'd better be wearing a suit."

"Is that why you went to law school? So that you could push back on racism?"

"It was really because of my dad. He was a machinist in the Emeryville shipyards during World War II. The guys all pitched in to make things work. Dad came up with some clever innovations. Didn't get credit for them—his white boss did. When I became a lawyer, I set up a *pro bono* program at my firm, helping inventors of color claim ownership for their work."

"That is cool. And your law firm supported you?"

"They did. The program is a great success. And now, if our invention succeeds, or my book sells..."

"Or both."

"...or both, I'd like to do something to commemorate my mom."

"What was she like?"

"Mom opened a hair salon after the war, down the block from Dad's car repair shop in the Fruitvale. You know that part of Oakland?"

"Sure. Great tacos."

Maxine smiled. "Yeah. Mom's salon was the meeting place for women from all over the neighborhood. Black and white, straight and queer—my mom believed in the power of women together."

"I'm starting to believe in that too."

"I'm glad. Brendan kept you down for too long."

"Yes. I let him keep me down. That's not a mistake I will make again. I'm very grateful to you and Joyce."

"You're not sorry you wrote to us?"

"Not anymore. But I did enjoy being with a man."

"Now you're scaring me."

"Hey, they can't all be like him."

"Amen to that."

* * *

Back in the 1860s, when Mark Twain wrote for the *San Francisco Daily Morning Call*, he called Emeryville, California "the most corrupt town west of the Mississippi." The dog racing track is long gone, though some of the card rooms remain. Gone too are the shipbuilding docks of World War II, and the motorcycle gangs that roamed the streets in the 1950s. Small superfund sites dot the landscape, mementoes of environmentally unfriendly companies that moved in after the war. The town leadership welcomed the next generation: computer and biotech firms that rehabilitated old factories and cleaned up the pollution in the ground.

Just in front of a busy railroad track at the edge of town was a small brick building with a sad little parking lot where weeds sprouted through cracked pavement. The relic once housed biocontainment labs for early research on HIV. That was back in the 1980s when there was no test to diagnose the virus, much less a way to treat it. Abandoned for many years but on valuable land, the building was home to rumors of ghosts, perhaps of the chimpanzees who gave their lives for AIDS research, or a lab worker who died there. Now the antique bricks were scheduled for demolition to make way for a state-of-the-art facility like the buildings nearby.

In that condemned building, Rose and Joyce supervised the installation of equipment in a rustic lab that clearly had not been touched in years. A cleaning crew was hard at work, and two guys were busy repairing the HVAC system.

Joyce was proud of their new quarters. "We'll have this up and running in no time."

"If you say so." Rose looked around. Hoses hung in untidy loops from the ceiling and partitions drooped.

"Come on," said Joyce. "Let's find a conference room and get to work."

Soon the two scientists stood at a whiteboard in an empty, partly lit room. On the board was the equation for photosynthesis. The women gestured and talked, while elsewhere in the building, workers brought the labs up to current standards.

Canopy Enterprises was launched. It was the first of June. They had exactly twelve months to make magic happen.

* * *

A week later, Joyce, Rose and Maxine met in that same conference room. By then all the lights were working and the room boasted a small table with six chairs.

Joyce was at the board. "I'll modify algae and plankton genomes to test various improvements to photosynthesis. One avenue we'll explore is alternatives to chlorophyll. I'm using a matrix design, testing select combinations of variables to get the biggest bang from our research bucks."

"Great!" Rose stood and joined her. "I'll supervise a team of interns to grow up your leading contenders for testing. Two of my best students, Isis and Marisol, will join us full time for the summer."

Maxine nodded. "Excellent. My friend Gloria is a partner at my old firm. She's on sabbatical this summer and offered to help. Plus she lined up two law students to start drafting patents on their summer break. Let's make sure they have something to write about. And I'll look for bioengineering interns to test materials for the shell panels." Maxine consulted her notes. "We also need to talk about IT support. There's a proposal we should consider. Rose, do you have time to meet with the guy?"

"Sure, I can do it next week, while Joyce is in early stages."

"Thanks. Once we have our first provisional patent, I can talk with our venture capital friends on Sand Hill Road. But if we're careful, we should last a year before we need outside funding."

Joyce crossed her fingers. "We should have great data by then."

After the meeting Rose and Joyce walked back to the lab.

Rose was in a contemplative mood. "Funny, isn't it?"

"What?"

"I feel so confident about this venture, even though it's a huge gamble. I've never felt that way about a relationship."

Joyce stopped and looked at her. "I understand those feelings, even though they aren't logical. What we are doing here could change a lot of people's lives. And romance is just—romance."

"Brendan told me once that I confused ice cream with oxygen."

"Indeed. So let's go make some oxygen."

* * *

Gloria and her legal interns were seated in the conference room when Joyce and Rose walked in. "Glad you could join our patent meeting. I'd like you to meet Simone and Kevin, our patent clerks for the summer. We've talked about the world of tech startups, and how it's lean and mean when it comes to amenities. The focus is on topflight work, and based on that, these two should fit right in. Simone, Kevin, please introduce yourselves to Joyce and Rose, two of Canopy's founders and our lead inventors."

Simone reached across the table to shake hands. "I'm Simone Garcia, a first-year student at Berkeley Law, where I also did my undergrad in Botany. I've known for years about Maxine Vargas' *pro bono* patent program at Stilton Ramsey, and I'd like to join that project after law school."

Gloria nodded. "Thanks Simone, I'll make sure Maxine knows about your interest — and it's great to have a botanist on board. How about you, Kevin?"

"I'm Kevin Welch, second year law at Berkeley. My undergrad was in engineering, and I'm super excited about working on these advanced solar panels."

"Terrific," said Gloria, "Thank you both. Your undergraduate backgrounds make you great candidates for patent work. And now please indulge my introduction to patents. It may be old hat to some of you. Joyce, you come from a biotech background, don't you?" Gloria could not help but notice the buff muscles under the lab coat of the woman across the table.

"Yes, I ran a research lab at Sirona here in Emeryville before Maxine, Rose and I started Canopy."

"So some of this will be familiar. Whereas Simone won't have encountered patent law yet, coming off her first year of law school. So let's make sure we are on the same page."

Gloria turned on an overhead projector and began showing slides. First was a person in Renaissance robes surrounded by antique books and labware. "Let's face it: patent lawyers are Renaissance humans. We have to know science, and the law, and how to write. Both of you law clerks are on your way, and this summer will give you a boost. Take a look." Gloria's next slide showed a ranch surrounded by fences. "A patent is like a fence you put around an invention, to show that you own it. And the bigger the area you can fence in, the better. But that analogy gets complicated because there are several kinds of patents. We will use different ones for different parts of the Canopy Roof System. By the time we are through, we won't just have a regular fence. We'll have the legal equivalent of an electrified fence with a moat." Her audience chuckled at Gloria's next slide, a medieval castle surrounded by a deep moat and some very modern fencing. "The first patent type we will use is a plant patent, for newly invented plant organisms. Simone, our botanist, you'll work with Rose on that one, including the drawings and botanical descriptions for our modified algae. We'll do more if we add other plants."

"Perfect." Simone looked up from taking notes and Rose gave her a thumbs up.

"The second type is a design patent that covers the look of the solar panels, including the outer materials and the algae farm inside each one. Kevin, our engineer, you'll draft patent applications of that type."

Kevin grinned. "Thanks Gloria, that sounds great."

Gloria continued. "I will start on the provisional patents for the roof system with specifications and drawings. At Stilton Ramsey I'm a litigator, so I'll be on a steep learning curve too. Maxine Vargas is the master drafter, and I'll go to her with questions. And I will ask each of you for technical support as needed. Labs in other companies are working on competing ideas, so the key is to get our patents filed as soon as we can. The filing date establishes ownership. And I can't stress this too strongly: We cannot discuss our inventions publicly until we file. No publications, Rose and Joyce, at least not until our provisional patents are filed. No interviews, no chats with investors. No bragging to our scientist friends or even to our moms. Everyone here has signed a Nondisclosure Agreement, and the consequences of letting the cat out of the bag are dire. We could lose ownership of everything we develop. Understood?"

Everyone in the room nodded.

"Good. I'm on sabbatical from the law firm, so I'll be here to support you every step of the way. Kevin and Simone, our lab scientists will become your best friends. And you'll also get to know Maxine, our company president, who trained as an engineer before she became a patent lawyer."

Simone looked thrilled. "Thanks Gloria, what a great opportunity. This will be quite the summer."

Kevin looked serious. "We're on it."

L ater that day, Rose stood at the lab bench with her former students, Isis and Marisol. All three women wore lab coats and goggles. "A big welcome to you both. You're joining Canopy at a challenging time, and the stakes could not be higher."

"Yes." Isis nodded. "We already met with Gloria and signed Nondisclosure Agreements. We know how important confidentiality is."

"Terrific. We're going to need all your good ideas, but just among ourselves. It will take a lot of hard work. I hope you're both prepared for some late nights this summer. I'm sorry we can't pay you. But if we succeed, we will all be well rewarded."

"We're ready for it," said Marisol. "That's why we are here. Working with you is already a reward, Dr. Bingham."

"Thanks, Marisol. That's very kind. And none of that 'Doctor' stuff here at Canopy. We are colleagues now. Both of you please call me Rose."

Just then Joyce walked in. "And you can call me Joyce. Welcome, ladies! I suppose Rose has told you that we'll be living in the lab the next few months?"

"Yes, she has," said Isis. "It sounds great!"

"Excellent," said Joyce. "Let's get started."

CONTACTS AND CONTRACTS

U nlike her corporate colleagues, Rose was accustomed to Spartan quarters. The tight fit of desk and chair in her new office did not concern her. What did bother her no end was the intransigence of her computer. Good thing her office lacked a window—she might have tossed the laptop into the parking lot. She may, in fact, have uttered a few choice Anglo-Saxon monosyllables just as someone entered the room through the door behind her.

"Step away from the computer," said a man's voice.

"What?" Rose jumped several inches. As startled as she was, she still noticed the man had a Michael Caine English accent.

"Always glad to rescue a damsel in electronic distress."

"Have you signed a Non-Disclosure Agreement? You can't look at this!" Rose blocked the screen with her hands.

"Sure I can. And it won't mean a thing. I hated biology. Almost as much as you hate computers." He spoke in a soft, ironic tone. He could have read a page from the dictionary and made it fascinating. She turned and saw a compact Englishman with salt and pepper hair and a handsome, lived-in face.

Standing, she put her hands on her hips. "Who are you?"

"Do you always start meetings this way?" He held out his hand. "I'm Nash Wiggins, IT consultant. I'm here to solve your computer problems, and any other gadget issues that might arise."

"Oh. Sorry. Thanks. Can you fix lab equipment too?"

"Of course. Useful sort to have around, me."

Rose stood and gestured for Nash to take her seat. "Why, thank you, Ma'am," he said, and then opened and closed screen windows with alacrity.

"The machines cannot win. We won't let them," he mumbled.

Rose would have stepped back, but there was no room. Instead she watched the upward turn of his shoulders as he worked. He talked, mostly to himself, cajoling her machine into good behavior. "Come on, baby."

For just an instant, before she stopped herself, Rose imagined Nash Wiggins hovering over her, saying just those words.

* * *

Three weeks later, Rose and Joyce stood at the whiteboard in Joyce's lab while Joyce gave an update.

"We've boosted CO_2 capture by changing the intermediates in the reaction, using both algae and phytoplankton as hosts. Not optimal yet, and we're struggling on the energy production side..." Joyce gave up trying to talk over the noise of a floor-cleaning robot that entered the lab, followed by a man Joyce did not recognize.

"Good morning, ladies," he said, sounding quite British. "This thing works much better now that I've cleaned its bottom. I knew you had to do that for small children. Didn't know you had to do it for robots."

The squat robot spun its way out of the room with the man following. Rose stared at the doorway after they departed.

Joyce turned to Rose. "Who was that?"

Rose blushed. "That's Nash, the new IT guy. He fixes other things besides computers, apparently."

"You look intrigued. Are you going to let him fix you, too?"

"Joyce!"

"Just remember the difference between ice cream and oxygen."

"Yes, I know. I'm on a strict oxygen diet."

* * *

Stephanie opened the door to her therapy office. "Welcome back, Rose. Good to see you again."

Rose took a seat and told the story of meeting Nash, and her instant attraction to him.

"I'm not ready to date, but I won't be able to avoid him. He's a consultant to my company."

Stephanie smiled. "You were taken in by Brendan, a sophisticated narcissist. That doesn't mean you have to avoid every man who attracts you for the rest of your life. But on the other hand, nor do you need to act on your attraction. Keep it simple. Acknowledge your interest in Nash, just in your own mind, and live your life. He's your colleague. Work with him. That's all. That's the nature of this relationship."

"Thanks." Rose nodded. "I get it. I think I can do that."

* * *

Maxine and Gloria fit in Maxine's small, undecorated office at Canopy Enterprises without much room to spare. It was not the kind of digs they were used to, and she was glad that Gloria took it in stride. "I'm impressed with the law students you've referred to us. They came by and introduced themselves after your patent meeting."

Gloria nodded. "Glad to hear that. It's a real win-win: Simone and Kevin didn't get tapped for summer jobs at Stilton Ramsey, but they're smart and they'll do great work. And they will love having Canopy Enterprises on their resumes."

"Even though it's an unpaid internship."

"Oh, they'll get paid plenty once they graduate. Especially if they've helped draft some of the key patents of the century."

Maxine raised one eyebrow. "Don't jinx it."

Joyce wedged into the room and took the only other seat, right by the doorway.

Maxine looked up. "Joyce, I think you've met Gloria, a friend and fellow partner from my old law firm. She's the one who helped us find summer clerks to draft our patents."

No room to shake hands, so Joyce waved. "Yes, good to see you, Gloria. Many thanks for your help."

Gloria nodded. "Happy to assist you fine women with starting your company. It's a great cause. Right now I need to get back and wrap things up at Stilton Ramsey. You'll have my full attention starting Monday. 'Bye Max. Joyce, it's a pleasure to see you."

"And you too."

Gloria tried to slip past Joyce in the tight space. Joyce had to stand so Gloria could pass and they locked eyes.

"Excuse me," said Gloria.

"Quite alright." Joyce caught her breath as Gloria's ample breasts brushed against hers in passing.

Maxine observed the moment. "She's a great friend. I miss working with her and I'm glad she is helping us out. I hope you and she get to know each other." *Even though,* thought Maxine, *Gloria claims she doesn't date colleagues.*

Joyce was blushing. "I hope so too."

* * *

J oyce stood at a tank in the lab, measuring the growth of intensely green algae modified to produce an electrical current. Rose walked in and Joyce glanced over, frowning. "We made so much progress at first."

"Beginner's luck. The growth rate isn't bad," said Rose. "And neither is the electrical production. It's just not fantastic."

"We're still ahead of what other people have published. But we don't know how much progress they have made since publication."

"True. We are just not where we want to be. Not when we're burning through cash."

The next day, Maxine, Joyce and Rose met in their monthly executive session, scoping out the competition.

Maxine launched right in. "I've reviewed the patents from other labs and emailed them to you. Take a look: Others have made progress with artificial photosynthesis, beefing up carbon dioxide conversion, but as far as we know, nobody has filed with an exovoltaic feature."

Rose boiled it down. "So nobody's generating electricity along with increased oxygen production."

"As far as we know." Maxine nodded.

Joyce looked up from her journals. "I've been reading the research papers and nothing there either. If we can get that to work, it's..."

"The Holy Grail," said Rose.

"The brass ring," said Joyce.

"The alpha and omega," said Maxine. "Pick your favorite cliché. Let's go do it."

* * *

And they did go do it, hour after hour, day after day. Two weeks went by.

"Dr. Bingham? Could you come into the lab? I have something to show you." From the look on Marisol's face, it was not something good.

"Call me Rose, please, Marisol. We talked about that. We are colleagues now."

"Maybe not for long." Marisol leaned over one of the tanks. "Here. It's my fault. I mixed up the solutions and now the plankton is incubating in the wrong fluids."

Rose took a look. "Nothing's dead yet. Remember when we talked about mistakes in class, Marisol? We don't know what kind of mistake this will turn out to be. Give it a few days. Let's see how it plays out."

"Aren't you worried? I know we're not flush for cash."

"Hang in there, Marisol. We're not up against it yet. But we are all tired, and this kind of thing will keep happening if we don't take care of ourselves. How long have you been here today?"

"Since six this morning."

"That's thirteen hours. Go home and get some sleep, please."

"Will you let me back in tomorrow?"

Rose smiled. "Of course we will. Be nice to yourself. Eat some vegetables and get some rest."

Marisol nodded, looking slightly less glum, and headed home.

* * *

Three days later Rose knocked on the open door of Joyce's office. "Could you come into my lab for a minute? Marisol and I have something to confess."

"Oh?" That sounded menacing enough for Joyce to interrupt her data review. She followed Rose back to the lab, where Marisol was waiting.

The three of them stood around the big tank, where Rose began their impromptu meeting. "Listen, Joyce, we made a mistake."

Marisol cleared her throat. "Actually, I made a mistake."

"Alright, Marisol, don't take all the credit. You wanted to dump the tank. I told you not to." Rose turned to her business partner.

"Joyce, we grew some of your modified plankton in the wrong solution. That should have killed it but look at it."

They all looked. The tank was lush and green.

"This stuff is making oxygen at four hundred times the rate of unmodified photosynthesis."

"Wow! That's fantastic!"

"Yes. It's better than anything in the literature. Better than any patent we have found."

"I'm impressed," said Joyce, "But this is just the beginning. Let's test this stuff at a variety of conditions and see how it responds. Right now you have it on a constant light supply. What happens when it gets as much light as a really sunny day?"

"We don't know yet," Rose said. "We will check that next. Marisol, onward!"

"Yes Dr.—Rose."

[13]

NEW AND IMPROVED

Gary was glad for a chance to eat dinner with Joyce, who was working long hours at her new company. The silver lining was that Gary had become a better cook. They sat down to his homemade ravioli, of which he was justly proud.

"This is delicious! Thanks so much, Gary."

"My pleasure. It's great to have you here with me for the evening."

"Great for me too. Forgot to mention, though, that I'll be home late tomorrow night."

Gary offered Joyce the grated parmesan. "An extra night at the lab? How's it going?"

"It's going really well. But I won't be at work. I'm having dinner with someone."

"Oh?" Gary's ears perked up. "What's his name?"

"Her name is Gloria." Just saying that name was electric.

"Too bad, I was hoping you'd met somebody. Someone who could make you happier than Brendan did. Although I realize that's a pretty low bar."

Joyce rolled her eyes. "Yes, it sure is. Way too low."

Gary smiled. "Well, girl time is important too."

* * *

The next evening, Joyce and Gloria were shown to a table at a venerable eatery in downtown Oakland. There was a festival atmosphere in the air, as artists and jewelers sold their wares at booths outside.

"I'm glad we could get together," said Joyce. "How long have you and Maxine been friends?"

"Twenty years, at least. I got to know her when she and her husband Charles split up. I had kind of a crush on her back then. But Maxine is one of those rare women who is only attracted to one gender."

"You think that's rare?"

Gloria nodded. "I do. A lot of women suppress the urge. But almost all women have it."

"Wow."

"Take you for example, Joyce. I'll bet you are more fluid than you realize."

"I'm married. To a man." Joyce twisted her napkin in her hands.

"I know. Maxine told me that you have an open relationship."

"That's true."

"And your husband takes full advantage, but you don't."

"No, not right now."

"You could double your chances by checking out the ladies. And I bet you'd like it." Gloria reached across the small table and took Joyce's hand.

Joyce looked surprised but she did not pull back. "Gloria, what will people think?"

"Why? Because we're older?"

"No, I..."

"Because I'm black and you're white?"

"Well, no, not that..."

"Or because you're wearing a wedding ring and I'm not?"

Joyce laughed. "I guess there's a good reason in there somewhere."

"Maybe not. We chemists have to stick together."

"You're a chemist? As well as a lawyer?"

"Chem was my undergrad major, and then I went to law school. All patent lawyers are scientists too." Gloria gestured with her free hand. "Look around, Joyce. We're in Oakland, the Lesbian capital of the universe. This restaurant is owned by a dyke couple who are older than we are. No one in this room will disapprove of you and I holding hands."

"If you're sure," said Joyce, giving Gloria's hand a squeeze.

"And after dinner, how about you come home with me. Let me show you. A little at a time. No pressure. See if you like loving a woman as much as I think you will."

"Alright, I'll stop by. Just for a little while."

* * *

"I need to call my husband and tell him that I'll be late." Joyce could tell that she sounded nervous, and that only made her more nervous.

Gloria nodded. "Of course. Do you need privacy? My study is through there."

"Oh, thank you."

Joyce closed the door of Gloria's study and made the call. She was not sure what to say, so she stuck with the basics. "Hi darling. I'm going to be later than I expected."

"Oh? Are you alright?"

"Yes, I'm fine. Gloria invited me to her house after dinner, and we're visiting. Not sure what time I'll be home."

"Alright, my love. Have a nice time. I'm off to bed soon—we'll chat in the morning. Goodnight."

Was he full of questions and biting his tongue? Or just taking what she said at face value? Joyce reminded herself that she was doing nothing wrong, just something unexpected. She walked back out to the living room.

Gloria smiled up from the couch. "Everything OK at home?"

"Yes, everything is fine." Joyce sat down next to Gloria. "I told him we were visiting. So let's see... I have so many questions... like, when was the first time you knew you were attracted to women?"

Gloria smiled and put her hand on Joyce's knee. "I'm much more interested in when you first knew you were attracted to women." She leaned over and kissed Joyce's lips. "Maybe it was tonight?"

As Gloria took Joyce in her arms, Joyce felt the warmth of Gloria's luxurious breasts. Gloria was so round and her body felt nothing like Gary's. Gloria actually felt more like Brendan. At that thought, Joyce pulled back.

"What is it? Do you want to take it slower?"

"It's just that... I'm not sure how to explain."

Gloria sat back and waited for Joyce to collect her thoughts.

"The softness of your body..."

"You're not used to that, are you? It's different to be with a woman."

"My husband Gary is long and lanky. Your body is nothing like his. But I used to go out with Brendan Burns, and he was round and soft, kind of like you."

"From what I know about Brendan, being compared with him is no compliment."

Joyce laughed at that. "True. The man is such an ass. But when you put your arms around me just now, I remembered the times Brendan and I enjoyed each other's company. And there were times like that. Funny, I try not to think about him that way."

Gloria nodded. "I get it. The end of a relationship, even a rotten one, is a loss. We try to protect ourselves."

Joyce squeezed Gloria's hand. "Thanks for listening."

"Of course. What are friends for? And I hope we will be friends, first of all."

"I'm sure we will." Joyce touched her forehead. "I'm so tired, suddenly."

"Understood. I'll walk you to your car. Have a good rest, and I hope to see you another time."

"I'd like that."

As she drove away, Joyce waved at Gloria in her rearview mirror. Did she want to see Gloria again? So much to think about.

* * *

The next morning, Maxine gazed at the plants in Rose's lab. "I'm glad we have crossed the first hurdle of improving photosynthesis."

Rose put down her pH meter. "What do you mean by 'first hurdle?'"

"Well, think about it: It's great that we can bind more CO_2 and liberate more O_2—"

"Yeah like by 400 times."

"...but how would you put that tank on somebody's roof? Without the roof collapsing? Water is damned heavy."

"True. But this is still pretty great."

Maxine nodded. "We should certainly file a patent on it. I'll talk with Gloria. But we haven't reached our goal."

"But how do you grow plants without water? Plant them in dirt? That's heavy too."

"Hey, we're smart," said Maxine. "We'll figure it out."

* * *

Rose and Joyce were huddled over data when Nash walked into the lab. "Get in gear, Dr. Bingham. The reservation is at noon."

Rose turned to Joyce. "I'll catch up with you after lunch."

"Sure," said Joyce. "After a big dish of ice cream, no doubt."

"Strictly business," said Rose.

"What's she talking about?" Nash whispered to Rose as they left the lab.

"Beats me." Rose shrugged. "You know... chemists."

They walked to a lunch place around the corner in a converted factory, with big windows and exposed brick walls, decorated with paintings by local artists.

"It's lovely of you to invite me to lunch, Nash."

"Oh yes, just lovely, that's me."

"No, it really is. I wasn't sure if you intended this to be a meeting, or maybe you don't want to talk shop. But I need to tell you that my work is all-consuming right now, until we can file our patents and protect our invention."

"You still need to eat."

"Yes, of course. I just mean I'm not ready for any kind of commitment right now. No serious relationship."

"I'm perfectly fine with a humorous relationship." Nash picked up his backpack and rooted around in it.

"What are you looking for?"

"A clown nose. Put in a little motor, they make pretty good vibrators."

Rose laughed and blushed. "So... no big love job?"

"As you wish. Just an unromantic bowl of soup. And these folks make an amusing crepe. Would you like one?"

"Yes, I believe I would."

Days later, Rose climbed the paneled stairway to Stephanie's Alameda office and knocked on the door.

"Come in, Rose. Glad to see you. How have you been?"

Rose sat down. "I'm doing well, but there's something I need to talk about."

Stephanie smiled. "Good thing, or the next hour would be awfully quiet. What's on your mind?"

"Remember when I told you about our IT consultant?"

"Nash—isn't that his name?"

"Yes. And you said the nature of that relationship was collegial, and I should acknowledge my feelings to myself and leave it at that."

"I do remember that. You came to see me initially out of concerns about your attachment to Brendan, a predatory narcissist. Well-founded concerns, in my view. And it seemed important for you to take time for yourself once that connection was over, to take stock of your own strengths and boundaries. Do you feel that you've done that?"

Rose shrugged. "I'm not sure how to tell."

"That's a good point. It's not like there is a litmus test. But tell me what is going on in your life, that prompts you to revisit your concerns."

"I've been getting to know Nash at work, and sometimes we have lunch together. He's not like Brendan at all. He's funny, and pokes fun at himself. He's smarter than he realizes, and he is genuinely impressed with the work my colleagues and I are doing. My radar says he is a good man, but I don't know whether or not to trust myself yet. And now I've gone and done it."

"Done what?"

"I've invited him to dinner. The last time I invited a man to dinner it was Brendan and it was a disaster."

"Take a deep breath, Rose. Inviting a man to dinner can mean nothing more than sharing a meal. You have grown and changed since Brendan, you are running a company now, and at least from what you have said so far, this man Nash does not sound like a pathological narcissist. Take it steady. If the evening is uncomfortable, find a reason to cut it short."

But as it turned out, the reason found Rose.

* * *

Nash arrived at Rose's front door bearing gifts. Juggling a plant and a bottle of champagne, he fidgeted on the porch like a teen on his first date.

Rose opened the door, smiling. "Hi. Come on in." The sight of the plant in his hands brought back unpleasant memories. *He's not Brendan*, Rose told herself. *It's not a bouquet. Nash means well.*

But what *was* that spindly looking thing he was holding?

"I brought you a housewarming gift." He held out the odd-looking plant proudly.

"I've lived here for months. By now my house is pretty warm."

"Yes, but this is my first visit. Hence the present. It's a *Tillandsia*."

"Should I get a vase? Or some dirt?"

"Neither one. Water drowns it and dirt kills it. It's called an air plant. It gets moisture from the air."

"Wait a minute." Rose sat down heavily, thinking. An air plant. No water, no dirt, just this very light plant. She stood up suddenly and kissed Nash on the cheek. "Gotta go."

"What? I was hoping we were in for a romantic evening. I brought champagne." He waved the bottle.

"Save it for next time," said Rose. "I'm taking your plant to Canopy. And thanks, by the way."

Nash shrugged. "This is what I get for falling for a nerd."

With that, Rose was out the door.

Back at the office, Rose dissected a thin sample from Nash's present and looked at it under the microscope. In the morning Joyce could sequence its genome. Meanwhile Rose read until the wee hours, everything she could find online about air plants, including that they really did need to be watered sometimes. "Joyce can fix that," Rose announced to the four walls of her office.

* * *

Later that morning Rose showed her new acquisition to Joyce and Maxine.

"Not to rain on your parade, but I've just met with Gloria," said Maxine. "She told me Simone has just submitted our modified plankton patent."

"All that work we did with plankton won't go to waste," said Rose. "What we need to do next is take what we've learned about improving photosynthesis and apply it to one of these air plants. I read up on them last night, and it looks like we have about 450 kinds to choose from, including mosses, ferns, lichens and orchids."

"And this inspiration is courtesy of your favorite IT guy, Nash," teased Maxine.

Rose decided to ignore that. "No water needed, as long as there's sufficient moisture in the air. And I'm betting Joyce can up that efficiency to cover dry climates. No dirt needed either, so we can grow these things on a tray of some kind."

"Sounds promising, Rose." Joyce was already on board. "In my lab, we'll work on the sequences needed to incorporate improved photosynthesis into the cells. And we will increase the moisture efficiency in the main genome."

"Great," said Rose. "Then in my lab we'll grow them to full size and see how they do."

Maxine nodded. "Sounds like you both have your work cut out for you. And I'll talk with Gloria about gearing up for another plant patent. Our legal team will be burning the midnight oil."

* * *

After an incredibly intense development phase, Joyce walked into a founder's meeting with Maxine and Rose. "We've got it. We have plants that get all their moisture from the air and still have increased photosynthesis. The efficiency dropped just a little to about a 350% increase over unmodified plants —still terrific."

Maxine applauded. "Fantastic! Now for the next step: Can we make them photovoltaic? These same plants that we've already messed with so much?"

Joyce smiled wryly. "Not asking for too much, are you?"

"Keep your eye on the prize, Joyce. Back to the lab with you. And you, too, Rose. Put Iris and Marisol to work on this one."

W eeks later, Rose knocked on Maxine's open door. "Got a minute?"

"Sure." Maxine looked up from her computer.

"Great. Do you want the good news or the bad news?

Maxine smiled. "Good news first. Always."

Rose gestured for Maxine to follow her. "Come with me and see."

Rose ushered Maxine into her lab, where Joyce was already hovering over a wire rack of spindly brilliant green plants. Metal clips attached to the rack carried current via wires to an ammeter. The needle measured a steady flow of current from the plants on the rack.

"Are you telling me that we have it? Photovoltaic plants that don't need dirt or water, and have exceptional photosynthesis?"

"Yes. We still need to up the electrical output per plant, but we are close to our specifications."

Maxine wanted to hug Rose but kept her professional restraint. "That is marvelous! Well done! I can't see any bad news here."

"Look a little closer."

Maxine looked at the rack of plants. "My only suggestion is, we'll need to increase the density and grow many more plants on a rack this size. It's not just electrical output per plant, we also have a goal for output per panel."

Joyce nodded. "Exactly. And that's the problem: These plants are so spindly, they take up a lot of horizontal space, and they don't like to touch each other. Their electrical output drops close to zero if they are near another plant."

"Are all *Tillandsia*s this picky about their neighbors?"

"No, not all of them. But this species was by far the easiest to manipulate genetically of the ones we tried. If we start over with another species, it will set us way back."

"And I don't suppose we have the resources to work on this species and another one in parallel."

Joyce shook her head. "You know the answer to that. Everyone is maxed out. No one takes weekends anymore."

"What do you want to do?"

Rose spoke up. "I had an idea for making a smaller version of these. I thought if we arrested their development at the point when they've just split off from a parent plant, what is called the pup stage, they would be more compact and we could set up an array with a lot more plants that were not touching."

"I like it." Maxine gave a thumbs up. "Let's try that."

"OK," said Joyce, "but first I need a nap. A long one."

[14]

DEATH AT THE POPCORN PALACE

That Kate character had vanished like a mirage. Finally agreed to meet for a date and then stood him up. Then not one more word, ever.

So be it. He had started over with women a dozen times. He could do it again.

Brendan talked out loud as he typed on his computer. His dating profile needed an update. "Suddenly single—ha!—serene smarty seeks intelligent but gullible women—no!—seeks one loving companion for evenings of scintillating conversation and quiet cuddles... Good grief that sounds boring."

But he posted it, boring or not, then waited for replies like a cat at a mouse hole. At his age, there were far more single women than men. The odds were in his favor.

He did not have to wait long.

* * *

Claudia wore a pink silk suit, very Chanel. She could tell that her date appreciated her clothes and what was in them. He had dressed for the evening too, a suit and tie that dignified his large frame. Dinner was delicious. He took her to a seafood place down the hill from Piedmont. They knew their way around the restaurant business: white tablecloths, a sommelier, the whole nine yards.

At first take, he was a cut above the usual dating website fodder. He was erudite if somewhat verbose, well versed in a variety of subjects. Claudia Chen never talked about the books in the pipeline, not until it was time to publicize, but she toyed with the idea of spilling the beans tonight. Her instincts told her this guy would be interested in Maxine's new project. Tempting, but no. She would keep Maxine's confidence. She talked up this year's publication list instead, like the professional she was.

He invited her home for a nightcap afterwards. Did people still say "nightcap?" He did, apparently. On an impulse she said yes.

She walked into the house and gave herself a tour. "Cute place!"

"Thanks," he said, clearing a used dish from the coffee table. "A bit of a mess. I'm working on several projects right now."

She walked through to the bedroom. "And wow, look at this ideogram on your bedspread."

Oh. Wait. Something stirred in Claudia's consciousness.

"That?" He walked into the bedroom, and suddenly looked weary. "Yes. It's the Chinese character for, ah, Beauty, and it suits you so well, lovely Claudia."

He was mansplaining to *her*, the daughter of Chinese immigrants, about a Chinese symbol on a bedspread. Wow. Claudia crossed her arms. "'Beauty,' is it? Not 'Wisdom?' Not 'Honesty?' Or 'Poetry?'"

Brendan frowned. "I beg your pardon. What on earth do you mean?"

He looked so affronted that she had to laugh. "Oh my, it really is you! I'm Maxine Vargas' editor at Dolphin Press. She's in contract with us for *Brilliant Charming Bastard*. I knew she based the Bastard on a real person, but what are the chances?"

"Indeed." Brendan crossed his arms. "What *are* the chances? What are the chances that four different women—you highly fungible beings—would challenge me—*me*? They say a man always remembers his first love, but after the first he tends to group them. And this group—this—*batch*—of you creatures has caused the most trouble in my entire existence." He was yelling now, redfaced. "Worthless ungrateful wretches, all of you. Not just the four of you. All of your kind."

"If you despise women that much, why so desperate for our company? And by the way, that character on your bed is the Chinese symbol for 'Liar.'" Claudia walked out of his bedroom, laughing, then out of the house, and slammed the front door behind her.

"Damnation," Brendan said to the silent walls. "What are the chances?"

* * *

There is a moment in romancing a woman that is like the reddest, sweetest bite at the center of a melon. It does not happen the first time in bed, or the second; possibly the sixth or the tenth, or more likely the twentieth time. Brendan always knew when it was coming, and it was his favorite time to film. A woman in that moment is not looking for cameras, not that any of them ever noticed the tell-tale blinking red light on his computer. And that sweet moment was the thing he most wanted to see afterwards, when a woman believed that she had left him.

Later that evening, still dressed in a suit from his unfortunate date with Claudia, Brendan loosened his tie and took three discs off the shelf from his Star Trek bootleg series. He inserted one into his DVD carousel—another relic, like him, he reflected. He flopped onto the couch, ready to enjoy himself. Damn them all, he was still king of his castle, with his remote control, his bowl of popcorn and a glass of red wine.

The archive system was simple. Hide in plain sight is best for such things. His special discs were mixed in with his collection of Star Trek episodes. Nobody was surprised he owned them, but nobody else really wanted to watch them either. Joyce, for example, was on the disc labeled "Plato's Stepchildren." Maxine was on "Catspaw." Both of those now sat on his coffee table. And Rose was, fittingly, on "Journey to Babel."

With his stocking feet on the coffee table and the remote control in one hand, he balanced the bowl of popcorn on his gut with the other. Rose was in the first slot on the machine. He pushed Play.

There she was, naked in his bed. Nervous, knowing what was coming, talking a mile a minute. He smiled.

"...and you know I really like it when you..."

"Rose," the recorded Brendan was saying on screen, "You are way overthinking this. Trust me. All you need to do is feel. Like this. Do you feel this?"

"Yes," she said, "Oh. Yes." Her voice became throaty with passion.

"And how about that?"

"Uh," she said, "Ah..." They always lose their consonants.

"Better," he said onscreen.

She was making sounds now, that singsong women make, when they go to that place where women go. He smiled on the couch, remembering. She looked like a professor but she fucked like a pro.

"Oh, Baby," Brendan was saying on screen. "That's it. You are doing great."

He remembered the feel of her seeking him, welcoming him. No matter how she moved, she could not get close enough. And her musky boxwood scent, how it filled him up.

"Time is an illusion," said the real Brendan, from the couch. "This is always happening, Rose. I'm still driving you." To boldly go... where no man had gone in years.

While Brendan ate his popcorn, Rose was rising in ecstasy onscreen. "Ah! Oh Brendan! Oh yes! Oh…"

Brendan watched avidly as his onscreen persona said, "Yes, Rose? You like that?"

"Yes! Oh I…"

With his mouth full of popcorn, Brendan said to the four walls, "You think you've left me, Rose? You think it's over? Time means nothing. It will never be over." He laughed and aspirated a kernel, stood, tried to cough, and pounded his chest. No good. Gasping but unable to take in air, he staggered to the dining room and rammed his ribcage into the corner of the table, over and over, trying to dislodge the blockage. He was so intent that he barely noticed when one of his ribs cracked. They might have thrown him out of medical school, but he remembered how this worked, this process of choking. He knew that next his trachea, trying in vain to push out the invader, would clench shut. Yes. There it was. Dear God. Must not panic. He tried to scream. Nothing. Must get help. Clutching his throat, Brendan half-ran, half fell toward the front door. His throat was burning now, right on schedule, terrible pain. Terrible. He landed flat on the carpet. He knew what came next. His brain, starved for oxygen, would secrete dopamine. He felt it kick in, just as expected. He was instantly calmer. That's why people liked erotic asphyxiation: a big dose of homemade happy drug. Things were progressing exactly as they should. The human body was a wonderful machine. Even now he could observe it. In spite of everything, science prevailed.

Brendan lost consciousness just as Rose reached her climax, loudly, on the screen.

* * *

The rental market in the East Bay heated up like crazy after the pandemic as tech workers rushed back from remote work in cheap places like Nevada and Idaho. Landlords were eager to show properties as soon as tenants left, whether they departed of their own free will or feet first. Business boomed for Tony Sturgis, who ran Clean at Last, a death cleaning business out of Oakland. It was even better when the dead were hoarders. The more crowded the house, the more hours and the more profit. And this old guy had been quite the packrat. Some good stuff mixed in, but most of it was total crap.

"Hey Tony!" The new guy, Wayne, called from across the living room. "You want me to keep these old paperbacks? Maybe they're worth something."

"Nah." Tony walked over to the shelves of yellowed science fiction. He had tried several times to sell boxes of paperbacks to used bookstores. "What you get won't pay for the gas to the bookstore. Recycle them."

"And what about these bootleg DVDs?"

"Nobody wants that crap. We might be able to get something for the player but ditch the bootleg."

"Will do." Wayne scooped the DVD cases with the handwritten labels off the shelf and the coffee table, and tossed them into a black plastic trash bag.

Tony walked into the bedroom to wipe the hard drive on the computer. It was a nice machine. That he could sell.

Tony shivered as he remembered what it was like in the pandemic. Going into homes where people died of COVID, knowing that their corpses could still be infectious, and the objects touched by the dead might be too. Working in body suits and respirators, scavenging the nice things like this computer, scrubbing down afterwards. It was tough sledding there for a while, but not anymore. The landlady told him how this one died.

Give me a good asphyxiation any day, he thought. *The old geezer choked to death on popcorn? Great.*

[15]

A DISCARDED DON JUAN

Maxine stood at the lab door and stared fixedly at Joyce and Rose.

Joyce was the first to look up. "What is it?"

"It's Brendan. He's dead. His funeral is tomorrow, I just saw the notice in the paper."

"What? You're kidding." Joyce put down her pipetter and looked at Rose across the room. "Rose? Did you hear that?"

"Yes." Rose was silent, arms folded. "I want to go."

"Why?" Maxine frowned. She had not expected that.

"I don't know. Closure, maybe." Rose looked up. "Will you two come with me?"

Maxine nodded. "Sure, I'll be there to support you. But I wouldn't go otherwise."

"I'll go too." Joyce looked at her friends and colleagues. "Here's what's weird: Without Brendan, I never would have met both of you. Or Gloria. Sure, I'm in."

"That's settled, then," said Maxine. "The ceremony is at one. We'll close the office at noon."

* * *

M oeser Lane is one of the steepest streets in the Bay Area, running up from the El Cerrito flats to the crest of the hills in the quaint town of Kensington. Standing at the top of the hills, the view is spectacular, from the downhill slope all the way out past the Golden Gate Bridge to the Pacific beyond. At the topmost point of Moeser Lane is the home of a congregation once known as the First Unitarian Church of Berkeley, which moved to Kensington in 1961 and declined to become the First Unitarian Church of Kensington (although certain wags enjoyed that acronym).

You might think that a church in such a setting would be all windows to allow in the sights, but you would be wrong. The church is a huge concrete bunker, a towering structure that could have accommodated great windows. But there are only a few slits of glass high up where no glimpse of bay or hills appears, just small bits of sky. The sanctuary is a vast aboveground cave, a place of silence and darkness. Rumor has it that the minister in charge when the church was built did not want to compete with the view for the attention of his congregants. That minister is long gone, but for better or worse, the eternal twilight remains.

Whatever truth may cling to those rumors, it is well documented that the congregation of this church pushed back against the Levering Act in the 1950s. That law required students to engage in Christian prayers in the public schools and required teachers and faculty members to take a loyalty oath to the United States government or lose their jobs. In 1954, ministers were notified they too must take the loyalty oath, or their churches would lose their tax exempt status. It was this church, the FUCK church, where the minister refused that oath. Along with two other brave congregations, the Kensington Unitarians took the case to the United States Supreme Court where the Levering Act was thrown out. In that moment, they showed the kind of spirit that makes Unitarian churches a favorite setting for memorial services of skeptics and scientists, whether they were kind and thoughtful in life or total knaves.

It was to this hallowed hall, this monument to many things (including male ego), that the mortal remains of Brendan Cantor Burns were brought for his memorial.

* * *

The sanctuary, that vast inverted battleship, was half full. Most people in the pews were women in their sixties and seventies. Near the chancel at the front of the church, a younger woman in ministerial robes greeted the mourners.

Rose, Maxine and Joyce sat near the back where they could observe quietly and leave if they chose. None of them had met anyone else in Brendan's circle. They wondered at the woman in the front pew wearing a pillbox hat and white gloves, dabbing her eyes with a handkerchief and speaking in quiet tones with the minister. Who was she? And who were the rest of these people?

Directly in front of Rose sat a woman in a bright red dress—defiantly not in mourning clothes. As they waited for the service to begin, she whispered loudly to the green-clad woman beside her, "...so I sprayed shaving cream all over her car."

"You didn't!" said her friend, directly in front of Maxine.

Maxine covered her mouth with one hand and gestured to Rose and Joyce with the other.

"I most certainly did. And I enjoyed it. You should have heard the noise from that house. Every night! I was sick of it. Could not get a good night's sleep in my own home."

"I'll bet it's quiet there now." The woman in green sounded grimly amused.

"It is bliss. Absolute bliss. I sleep like a baby."

"That was worth the price of admission, right there," Maxine whispered to her companions. "I bet half the women in this room are only here to make sure the bastard is dead."

"No," said Rose. "Way more than half."

"Hey, that's why I'm here," said Joyce.

As the last mourners were seated, the minister stepped to the pulpit.

"Good afternoon, and welcome to this beloved place. I am Reverend Trudy Sessions, minister of the church, and I welcome all of you, friends and family, to our service in memory of Brendan Cantor Burns. His sudden passing reminds us that life seldom ends neatly. We leave behind conversations never completed and projects half done. A memorial service is a time to speak well of the departed, to remember the best about the one who has gone on. But it is also a chance for the living to heal, to honor all that remains unfinished. At the time of his death, Brendan and his wife Margo Tanner—"

There were low murmurs from the pews. The woman in the pillbox hat turned around in the front pew and smiled vacuously at the assemblage. She gave a little wave with one gloved hand.

Reverend Sessions continued undeterred. "—Brendan and Margo were working toward reconciliation after a lengthy separation. We will hear from Margo later in the service. But first, Brendan's friend and research partner, Dr. Fred Hinkle, a professor from Palo Alto, would like to say a few words."

As a tall thin man with white hair stepped to the chancel, Maxine whispered to Joyce, "A professor from Palo Alto? He wants us to think he's at Stanford. What do you bet he's at some community college?"

"Don't diss community colleges," Rose whispered, and the brightly dressed ladies in the row ahead turned around and shushed them.

Fred Hinkle tapped the microphone and cleared his throat, his Adam's apple bobbing. He put a page of notes on the pulpit. "Thank you, Reverend. And thanks to all of you for being here. I see a few familiar faces and many who are new to me. Just shows how much Brendan was loved. And in addition to losing someone we care about, we have lost a truly original thinker—a great mind who was in the midst of creating a world changing invention. Our collaboration was one of the highlights of my life in science. Almost every time I saw Brendan or spoke with him, he had a new idea, a new angle on our work together."

"Yeah, I'll bet he did." Joyce leaned in to whisper.

Fred continued. "Brendan had a mind that was always searching. His is a great loss indeed. Let us honor him by continuing to explore our world and expand our understanding. Thank you and peace be with us all."

As Fred walked back to his seat, Reverend Sessions said, "Thank you, Dr. Hinkle. And now, a reading in memory of Brendan, from an old friend, Megan Hartshaw."

Megan was a short woman with big glasses. She came up from the second row of pews and stood at the pulpit looking sad and defiant. "I cared for Brendan but harbored no illusions. This poem by Edgar Lee Masters is spoken by the spirit of a man named Lucius Atherton, looking back on his life. I used to tease Brendan that he was channeling Lucius:

> When my mustache curled,
> And my hair was black,
> And I wore tight trousers
> And a diamond stud,
> I was an excellent knave of hearts and took many a
> trick.
> But when the gray hairs began to appear —
> Lo! a new generation of girls
> Laughed at me, not fearing me,
> And I had no more exciting adventures
> Wherein I was all but shot for a heartless devil,
> But only drabby affairs, warmed-over affairs
> Of other days and other men.
> And time went on until I lived at Mayer's
> restaurant... a gray, untidy,

Toothless, discarded, rural Don Juan....
There is a mighty shade here who sings
Of one named Beatrice;
And I see now that the force that made him great
Drove me to the dregs of life.

As Megan took her seat the murmurs from the assemblage had a slightly rebellious tone.

The Reverend stepped back to the pulpit. "Thank you, Megan, for that insightful tribute. Now I invite each of you to share. Brendan's departure was sudden, and this is a moment when you can say what you would have said to him, had you had the opportunity." Did Reverend Sessions know what she was inviting? One by one, the women in the pews stood, approached the wooden box that held the remains of Brendan Burns, and unburdened their spirits.

"Brendan, you made me feel guilty for wanting the least show of affection," said a woman in her seventies, wearing a large black hat.

A woman all in grey was next. "You denied saying the exact thing you told me hours before. You told me my memory was faulty. It wasn't. You made me feel crazy. I'm not."

Next was a big woman in a black and yellow floral dress. "Brendan left me the very day that my dog died. Can you imagine? That same day. Not a shred of sympathy."

And on it went.

Maxine, Joyce and Rose felt no need to take a turn. Standing in the reception room afterwards with wine glass in hand, Joyce said, "Do you think his wife has any idea how lucky she is that they didn't reconcile?"

"If she didn't know before, she does now." Rose looked grim.

"And what about that fellow Hinkle, going on and on about Brendan's original mind, always coming up with new ideas? As if he had any ideas of his own." Maxine shook her head. "Hey, I'm ready to get out of here when you two are."

"In a minute," said Rose. "I like your book title, Maxine. *Brilliant Charming Bastard*. He wasn't all bad. He was brilliant, sometimes."

"He was charming, too, at first," said Joyce.

"And what a bastard. Always," said Maxine. "But he brought us together. Here's to us. Cheers!"

They clinked glasses.

Fred Hinkle walked up to them. "You ladies seem unusually festive for such an occasion."

"Hello, Dr. Hinkle," said Maxine. "I'm Maxine Vargas, and these are my colleagues, Dr. Joyce Farrell and Dr. Rose Bingham."

"Very good to know you. And how did you doctors know Brendan?"

The women looked at one another for a split second before Rose, who could never hold her liquor, said, "We dated him."

Joyce nudged Rose and shook her head. Whatever Rose was about to add remained unsaid.

"I see," said Fred, who looked like he would rather not see.

Maxine tried changing the subject. "We work together. The three of us own a startup called Canopy, over in Emeryville."

"Canopy... I've not heard of it. Interesting name. What do you make?"

Joyce jumped in before Rose could open her mouth and destroy their intellectual property. "We'll be glad to discuss that once we have filed our first patents."

Fred folded his arms. "Understood. It's so important to protect our intellectual property. We must talk, when you're ready."

Hinkle prided himself on knowing everyone in Silicon Valley, including several reporters at the *Silicon News*. He placed a call on his way down the steps of the church. "Randy. Listen. I need you to find out what's happening at a woman-owned startup in Emeryville. A place called Canopy. I'm sure there is a story in it. Call me."

* * *

W ayne tossed the last bag into the dumpster in front of the old guy's house. It was a sad bunch of garbage: ratty underwear, rotten food, and the bootleg DVDs from the coffee table. Then he headed to University Avenue to see what he could get for the DVD carousel.

At the top of the Avenue near the Cal Berkeley campus is an assortment of restaurants where students and locals enjoy the cuisines of every country, from the pupusas of El Salvador to the adobo of the Philippines. Downhill, toward the Berkeley flats, the storefronts are dusty and could use a coat of paint. Several are used electronics shops, and it was to one of those that Wayne made his way.

"Wow. I haven't seen one of these carousels in ages," said the guy at the counter, who was maybe nineteen and geeky looking. Jake, his nametag said. The carousel was probably older than he was. For electronics gear, that's almost museum time. Jake looked up. "I'll give you ten bucks."

"You can have it for twenty. And I'll throw in the DVDs."

"No, actually, you'll have to take those out and recycle them. I have enough crap to dispose of. Oh, but wait, here's a bootleg Star Trek episode. I'll hang onto that." Jake actually smiled. "Here's fifteen bucks."

"Sold," said Wayne. Not much, but enough to buy a plate of masala dosa from the Indian place up the block.

16

YOU ARE BEING SERVED

 From the *Silicon News:*

Heard on the Road: A certain botanist and would-be inventor says three founders of an East Bay agbio startup got their launch on the couch of a now-deceased scientist. Are their ideas truly their own? Or did they borrow them from their shared sweetie before his untimely death? This is one for the books.... Stay Tuned!

L ike many startups, Canopy Enterprises had no receptionist, and the dark glass entrance was kept locked. Fred Hinkle stood at the door, tall and stooped over, in a white dress shirt and khaki pants. His Adam's apple bobbed nervously as he cupped hands over his eyes and tried to see into the building. Nothing doing. He buzzed the doorbell.

"Yes?" came a voice on the intercom.

"I'm here to see Maxine Vargas."

"Is she expecting you?"

"No, but tell her Brendan Burns' research partner is here. I'm sure she will see me."

He was right. In a minute a buzzer sounded and Fred was admitted to a tiny anteroom. Maxine came out and walked him to her office. "To what do we owe the pleasure of your visit, Fred?"

He could not stand people who were overly familiar. Given that Maxine only held a law degree and he was a Ph.D., she should refer to him as Dr. Hinkle. He gritted his teeth and decided to let it go for now. "I learned at Brendan Burn's funeral that all three founders of this company formerly dated my business partner."

Maxine gestured for Hinkle to sit in the chair across from her, as she sat down at her desk. "That's true. In fact, we dated him at the same time. He lied to all of us."

Fred looked grim. "So, your revenge is to steal the ideas of a dead inventor? Shame on you."

"Oh, come on, Fred."

"That's Dr. Hinkle to you."

Maxine shook her head. "Your buddy Brendan dated a biologist, a biochemist, and a patent lawyer with an engineering degree. He lied to each of us about the nature of the relationship. At the same time, he grilled us about photosynthesis, and apparently told you that our ideas were his. And in the process of being exploited by your friend, we became experts in the field. And that expertise belongs to us."

"Tell that to a judge."

"Really? You want to go there? Just a moment." Maxine picked up her office phone. "Gloria, could you come by my office? Won't take a minute. Thanks." She put down the phone. "I am 'of counsel' at Stilton Ramsey, which you may or may not know is the premier patent firm in the Bay Area. Gloria Padgett is a litigation partner there, though she is spending her sabbatical onsite with us at Canopy."

Gloria walked into the small room.

"Gloria, this is Fred Hinkle. Those of us who attended Brendan

Burns' memorial met Fred there. He was Brendan's research partner. Fred, please explain your bizarre theory to my attorney."

Fred snorted. "I won't waste my time. But you'll be hearing from me. And I'm not like Brendan Burns. You won't get around me with your wiles. I will not be seduced."

"Believe me, Fred, I am relieved to hear that. And the other founders will be too. Now I need to get back to work. Presumably so do you."

Hinkle stood. "Excuse me." He scooted past Gloria and walked out of the building.

"What was all that about?" Gloria stared after him.

"That arrogant fool thinks we stole Brendan's ideas, instead of the other way around."

"No one will represent him. He has no case."

"I hope you're right. Even so, he's trouble. The more he gossips, the greater the risk to our intellectual property."

"I can see that. We need to get the *Tillandsia* patent filed pronto. Brendan is bad news, even from the grave."

* * *

Across the bay from Berkeley and south of San Francisco is the city of Palo Alto, at the center of Silicon Valley and the high-tech world. And in Palo Alto, not far from Stanford University, is a single street called Sand Hill Road where the real estate costs more per square foot than in midtown Manhattan. Starting in the 1970s, venture capitalists interested in funding technology companies set up shop on that road and made a killing. Maxine knew the place very well, having represented many an inventor as they went hat in hand to venture capital firms in search of funding.

As soon as Simone and Gloria filed the provisional patent for modified *Tillandsia*, Maxine reached out to Gordon Hendricks, a venture capitalist she had known for years. He was an African American financier in his early sixties and a partner at Tarth Capital. Gordon was glad to get a phone call from Maxine and invited her to lunch, which she declined. "Just business," she said. Two days later he ushered her into his corner office.

Maxine smiled as she sat across from Gordon. He looked fine in his charcoal suit, leaning back in a red leather chair behind his luxurious desk. "It's been a long time. How are you doing?"

"I'm good, Maxine, thanks for asking. Last child from marriage number two is now in college. And wife number two eloped with her gynecologist. I could make all kinds of jokes about that, but I'll refrain."

"Oh, Gordon, I'm so sorry."

"Don't be. It was time. Life moves on." He leaned forward and put his hands on his desk. "Now tell me about you, Maxine. How have you been? I heard you retired from Stilton Ramsey. Congratulations."

"Thanks. But I wouldn't call running a startup 'retirement.'"

Gordon laughed. "Neither would I. Although it must have put a few dollars in your pocket when the firm bought back your partnership."

"Yes, that will help, when the firm decides to part with the money. Assuming I can hang onto it."

"Your new company needs cash?"

"My new company needs cash. Which is why I'm here on business, and not just to see you, lovely as that is."

"Sure. So let's get to it: What's your burn rate?"

"Right now it's seventy thousand a month."

"Whoa. That's all?"

"That's all. We have free rent in an old lab building for a year, and the founders don't take salaries. We have several unpaid interns. We pay a few contractors and buy research equipment and supplies. Plus insurance and utilities. It's a lean machine."

"Amazing. And how much cash in the bank?"

"After set-up costs, we have just under a million. Not much. Our costs are low for now, but I'm thinking ahead. We'll have to start paying people soon. Building prototypes and setting up manufacturing agreements will cost us. Add on moving and rent, and our burn rate will go way up."

"How much are you looking to fund? Assuming you hang onto your partnership stash."

"If we take another year to reach a saleable invention, we will need another five million."

Gordon nodded. "Reasonable. How is your research going?"

"The first results are promising, but the devil is in the details."

"How true that is. I'd like to help you. And I'm sure my partners would too. But you don't have proven results yet."

Maxine smiled. "If we had proven results, we would be looking for a stock offering, not expensive private money like yours. People who don't need money have no trouble getting it."

"Touché."

"Think of it this way: Canopy is run by a full UC Berkeley professor, a Research VP from a publicly held biotech company, and me, a partner from the top patent firm in the Bay, who also trained in engineering. If three men with those credentials asked for seed capital, would you even hesitate?"

Gordon shook his head. "Max, we've done lots of deals on the same side of the table. I know your skills and how hard you work. Our concern is not your gender."

"Then what is it?"

Gordon looked uncomfortable. "I have to say that some difficult stories are circulating about Canopy."

"Oh? Like what?"

"I'm hearing your concepts may not be your own. That you got them via a back channel from an inventor who is deceased and can't defend his intellectual property. None of this sounds like the Maxine Vargas I know. But I have to ask you: Did you know Brendan Burns?"

"I knew him. I dated him briefly."

"The *Silicon News* claims three women stole ideas from a scientist before he died."

I take it Fred Hinkle is behind these rumors?"

"I can't comment. Although I hear that a story is coming out soon in the *Silicon News*. You can see how this puts us in a tough spot. Your company has promise if it has the potential for defensible patents. But that's your only asset and right now it's intangible."

"If this claim had any basis, Canopy would be hearing from Hinkle's lawyers."

"No lawyer will go up against a Stilton Ramsey partner unless there is airtight evidence."

"And there is none. Hinkle's story is a fairy tale."

"So where does that leave us?"

"That's my question for you."

"Let me talk with my partners. We will be in touch, Max. Good to see you." Gordon stood up to walk her out. Maxine wanted this to be a business meeting. And if business was all they could talk about, then the meeting was over.

* * *

The days fell from the calendar faster than a time lapse in a 1950s movie. Summer ended, and with it, the internships of Isis, Marisol, Simone and Kevin. No room at Canopy was big enough for the going away party, so the interns, the founders and Nash gathered for cake at a table behind the building. Fire season had started, and the afternoon sun was red from the smoke of fires up north in Napa.

"I am so proud of the great work that all of you have done this summer," said Maxine. "We're all grateful. And I seriously don't know what we will do without you. But every one of us wishes you the best this year at school."

Isis looked at her fellow interns, who nodded to her, and she stepped forward. "We've talked it over and we would like to stay on, part time, even after school starts. We'll set up a schedule and stick to it as best we can, even the law school interns, who have it much rougher than Marisol and I do."

Joyce felt a bit weepy. "That's amazing! Thank you so much for the offer. But we don't want to interfere with your schoolwork."

Isis shook her head. "What you're doing at Canopy is more important than school. It's about the future of the planet. We want to keep being part of it."

Kevin nodded. "Isis is right. I've wanted to be a lawyer all my life, and here I am standing outside with you breathing smoke from the fires. What kind of career will I have, what kind of lives will our generation have, if we don't do this work?

Rose shook Isis' hand. "How wonderful. We'll accept. On the condition that you will be paid, from now on."

Nash chimed in from the back of the group. "Attention Interns! Never leave money on the table! That's a rule."

Isis laughed and looked at the others, who nodded. "Alright. You're on."

* * *

At last Joyce was ready to report back to Rose and Maxine about their latest hurdle. "We now have a batch of pup plants that we believe will never mature. They will stay small and compact, and we can position them close together on a wire rack to maximize output per tray."

Maxine grinned. "That is fabulous! Do they still do what we want them to do? Photosynthesize hyper-efficiently? Produce electricity? Live on just air with no added water?"

"Yes. An array of these plants meets all our specifications. Now all we have to do is wait and make sure these traits persist."

Maxine folded her arms. "Well, no."

"What do you mean, 'no'?"

"That's not all we need to do. It's great that this system works indoors, in a lab. It's fantastic that we have a rough prototype. But we need to start thinking about real life conditions. You're going to put an array of plants on somebody's roof that will drown the first time it rains?"

"No, of course not." Joyce shook her head. "So we need a new stage of specifications, don't we?"

"Yes, that's right. We need a working model that we can put on a roof."

"The roof of the Canopy building?"

"Maybe not. Maybe we don't want somewhere that obvious. Maybe we want a roof that our old buddy Fred won't think to look at."

And that is when Rose visited Nash's house for strictly business reasons.

Nash opened the door. "Back when I brought you that *Tillandsia*, I was hoping to spend an evening necking on your couch. I didn't expect you to turn around and bring me a whole flat of the things."

Rose smiled and held out a tray of pup stage plants. "Nash, we all really appreciate your willingness to host this test on your roof."

"Of course! What would you like me to do with it?"

"Just keep an eye on it. Check it every day and see if it looks healthy, like it does right now. And I'll check too, a couple times a week."

Nash considered the tray of plants. "I read up about these air plants. They do need watering every now and then, despite their name. How would you like me to handle that?"

Rose shook her head. "These particular *Tillandsia* don't need watering."

Nash stared at her for a second. "You nerdy women did that? You made these plants better at pulling water from the air?"

"Yes."

"What else did you do to them?"

"We made them smaller so more of them could fit on an array. That way they can make more electricity per panel. And we did some other stuff."

"Other stuff like what? They're not carnivorous, are they?"

Rose laughed. "No. Not even close."

"Because I might be upset if they crawled through my window and ate my face."

"You'll be fine. Just check with Joyce or me if they don't look healthy."

For now they were almost preternaturally healthy. The compact plants looked more like succulents than air plants. They were a brilliant Viridian green, so intense that the human retina could not quite process the color. To look at these plants too long was to fall into a miniature primordial forest where tiny dinosaurs might break from the foliage at any moment. No wonder Rose liked them. Nash made himself look away.

* * *

A few days later, Rose saw Nash in the hall at Canopy headquarters. "How are our favorite plants doing?"

"They look great. In fact, they are flowering. I didn't know *Tillandsia* did that very often."

Rose frowned. "They don't. The mature plants only flower just before they make their offshoot plants, called pups, and then they die. I don't get it. We arrested their development just beyond the pup stage, so we could mount them close together. No way should they be flowering.'

"Here." Nash showed Rose a picture on his phone.

"No doubt about it. May I show this to Joyce?" Rose held out her hand for his cell phone.

"I can text it to you."

"Just come with me, in case my phone is tapped."

"Who would do that?"

"Our buddy Fred Hinkle."

"Rose, you're being paranoid."

She shook her head. "No I'm not. Just careful."

Rose gestured to Nash to hold out his phone. "Joyce, take a look at Nash's picture."

Joyce stared at the screen. "Flowers. Hell. Does this mean they're going to die?"

"Not long from now, yes. We'll have to try a different modification. And even if flowering didn't kill these plants, we don't want people to be able to grow our invention for themselves. Flowering means reproduction. We only want the Canopy invention to come from master stock owned by the company."

"Greedy aren't you?" Nash looked amused. "I admire that in a woman."

Rose frowned. "We want to protect our intellectual property. That's true. But also, these plants should be used as intended. We're not comfortable with them growing in the wild and outcompeting natural plants, which they would if they were out loose. They could overrun the biosphere. We want to save the planet, not wreck it."

Joyce sighed. "So many changes. One on top of the other. How can we begin to know how they all interact? And how many more problems will we find? And how long will it take?"

The clock was ticking.

* * *

"It's high time I introduced you to my favorite bar," said Rose, as she and Nash clinked beakers at The Lab. Around them the denizens of the Emeryville biotech scene were similarly engaged, talking with colleagues and drinking from glasses marked in milliliters.

Nash looked at the beaker in his hand, then looked around. "You would think some folks would get enough of lab glass during the day."

Rose smiled. "These are dedicated nerds, Nash. You're surrounded by them."

"Don't I know it. I work with some of the nerdiest nerds around. Who else would try to stop climate change from a funky little brick building?"

"It sounds terribly grandiose, when you put it that way."

"I don't think so." Nash became serious. "I think it's incredibly noble, and important."

"Thanks. It's a big project for three little old ladies."

"That's not who you are." He waved his arms. "You're a trio of Amazons. Valkyries. Warrior Queens." Rose was laughing at him. "What's so funny?"

"You are."

"I'm serious! You're my sheroes. Especially you, Rose. I've taken a bit of a shine to you."

"I kind of got that." Rose smiled.

"I know you're still reeling after that wanker Brendan lied to you and then kicked the bucket. But I'm not him."

"You're not like him at all. You're funny and sweet and kind."

He blushed a little. "No, not really. I'm OK, though."

Rose kissed him.

"What was that for?"

"For saying I'm a Warrior Queen."

"Then I might say it more often. But you don't have to remind me, I know: no big love job."

"No. No big love job."

Just then Rose's phone buzzed. She looked at the screen and frowned. "I need to get back to Canopy."

"What's wrong?"

"Maxine was just served court papers. Fred Hinkle is suing us."

17

AN EQUAL AND OPPOSITE REACTION

From the *Silicon News*:

Heard on the Road: Somebody is suing somebody. Sure, you say, somebody is always suing somebody. But this time it's sex, money, death, and nerds behaving badly—all rolled up into one not-so-neat package. Interested? Stay tuned...

The light was on late in the small conference room at Canopy Enterprises where Gloria had summoned the Canopy founders. Joyce was the first to join her. "How have you been?"

"I've been better." Gloria did not look well rested.

"And to think you could have spent your sabbatical on a beach somewhere."

"Yeah, a beach where the water level is rising from climate change. We've got to do something to help this world get right."

Joyce put her hand on Gloria's arm. "It's great that you're helping us. And listen, when this crazy lawsuit is over..." Gloria looked up at Joyce. Just then Maxine walked in, followed by Rose, and Joyce let go of Gloria's arm. The four women huddled around the conference table in the silent night, coffee mugs in hand.

"I wasted my time at Tarth Capital." Maxine shook her head. "They won't give us a dime while this lawsuit is pending."

Rose looked at Gloria. "I'm amazed that Fred found a lawyer."

Gloria gazed at the downcast women around the table. "I am too. But Jim Townsend is an ambitious young man, out to make a name with a high-profile case, even one that's sure to lose. I'll examine what they filed. From everything I know about your work here at Canopy, this has to be a nuisance suit."

"That's right." Maxine looked grim. "Fred will likely make a settlement offer quickly. Maybe a lump sum, maybe a share of our eventual earnings."

"No way we settle." Mild-mannered Rose was almost yelling. "Not one dime. Let's go all the way to court."

"That's not his game, though," said Gloria. "His story is just conjecture. It will all be innuendo, raising doubts with investors like Gordon. He knows you are a small company without much capital and he's playing you for time. He wants you to run out of funds so you have to settle."

"So he's blackmailing us." Rose looked disgusted.

"In essence, yes," said Maxine.

"Is that legal?

"Perfectly."

Joyce drummed her fingers on the Formica conference table. "If we could get to Brendan's computer..."

Maxine shook her head. "We looked into that. The house was a rental, and the landlady was in a big hurry to rent it out again. His drive was wiped before his computer was sold. His paper files were recycled."

Joyce poured more coffee. "Do you think this Hinkle guy believes what he's saying? Maybe we should meet and explain what really happened, that Brendan was stealing *our* ideas."

"I don't think so, Joyce." Maxine shook her head. "He's not going to believe three women over his dead friend who kept sending him material for their project."

Gloria looked at her companions. "What about your emails? Did the three of you send Brendan useful information about photosynthesis? Or solar power? Or did you only share ideas in conversation?"

"I sent him research articles with comments pretty frequently," said Rose.

Joyce nodded. "I sent a few."

"Good point," said Maxine. "I could check, maybe there's something. And look at it from the other side: he never sent us one word about his supposed invention."

"All of you, forward me whatever you've got," said Gloria. "And don't erase any emails between you and Brendan, no matter how embarrassing they look now. It's all evidence."

"Maxine already made us promise to keep everything, as material for her novel. Otherwise, I would have erased those emails already." Rose shook her head. "The farther I get from that relationship, the more disgusting it seems."

"Her novel..." repeated Gloria. "Now there's a thought. Maxine, how much of that book have you written?"

"I have seven chapters in decent shape. The first third of the novel. By the time I wrote those, Canopy was so busy that I stalled out. Why?"

"Let's sit down with your publisher. I have an idea."

* * *

A t the Berkeley Marina is a walking trail that runs parallel to the winding edge of the bay. Benches are strategically placed for hikers to pause and contemplate the San Francisco skyline across the water. To the right of the city is the Golden Gate Bridge and beyond it the blue Pacific. Farther right is the town of Sausalito, with Marin County and the wine country to the north.

On a balmy Saturday morning, Gloria, Maxine and Claudia, in

sneakers and hiking clothes, sat on a bench at the waterfront facing the bay. The sky was bright blue over the water, and the city skyline was wrapped in translucent fog.

Claudia stretched out her legs and crossed them at the ankles. "Maxine, did I ever tell you that I went on a date with him?"

Maxine, startled, turned away from the view to look at Claudia. "Went on a date with whom?"

"The Bastard. It was just before he died."

"You're kidding. What are the chances?"

"Exactly." Claudia laughed. "That's just what I said."

Maxine was intrigued but repulsed. "How did it happen?"

"I ran into him on a dating website. Those sites are like the last day of a yard sale. You never know what you will find."

Gloria shook her head. "Who didn't date that guy? Besides me, of course. What was he like?"

"Brendan was utterly charming at dinner. Then we went back to his place, and I saw the Chinese character on his comforter. He tried to tell me what it said, and of course I knew he was wrong. That is when it dawned on me that he had to be the real-life Brilliant Charming Bastard."

"Amazing." Maxine shook her head.

Claudia nodded. "It was quite a coincidence. And I believe that date was the night he died."

Gloria stared at her with eyes wide. "Claudia, you're not telling us that you..."

Claudia laughed. "Good heavens no! He was hale and hearty, if a bit peeved, when I walked out. But I'm not sorry he's gone, aside from his value as a source of story lines."

"He seems to generate conflict even from underground," said Maxine.

"Really?" Claudia was all ears. "Tell me about it. You know how I love a good story."

"Brendan's research partner Fred Hinkle, who spoke at his

memorial, believes that Brendan is the most original thinker he's ever known."

"Seriously? That is rich."

"Yes. And now Hinkle is accusing Rose, Joyce and me of ripping off Brendan's ideas for our company. He thinks our invention is really Brendan's. And his."

Claudia shook her head. "I don't suppose you want to join forces and offer him a job?"

"Absolutely not!" Maxine was adamant. "Brendan stole our ideas, not the other way around. We can't reward his collaborator, even if Fred believes that Brendan was the source of our ideas. But we have no clue what he really believes."

Gloria picked up the thread. "And this is where you come in, Claudia."

Claudia looked skeptical. "I'm a publisher, not a lawyer. What can I do?"

"Fred has been badmouthing Canopy Enterprises to potential investors. He's spreading rumors, and now he's filed a lawsuit. So far, the investors only have his side of the story. But we know he has no case. If the courts were not backlogged, we could just wait it out and tell our side in court. But Canopy is a small company and that wait could ruin us." A breeze picked up and Gloria folded her arms. "We need a different way to get the story out, before Canopy runs out of funds."

"I'd like to help you," said Claudia. "If Maxine could finish her novel, even a rough draft, I could fast track publication. I would put one of my editors to work on it right away or edit it myself."

"I'd love to oblige, Claudia, but I have no time to write. Running Canopy is taking all the bandwidth I have." Indeed, Maxine looked tired. "But as we've discussed, the first third of the book is in good shape."

Gloria continued her pitch. "Claudia, we would like you to begin releasing Maxine's novel in serial form."

Claudia's eyes widened. "Now that's interesting. Like they did in the eighteen hundreds. Like Mark Twain and Charles Dickens."

Maxine nodded. "Yes, and some modern writers do it too. Stephen King, for one. If we made some of the chapters available ahead of publication, as a teaser, it could end up boosting sales of the novel."

"Yes, it could." Claudia nodded agreement. "And I see how it would give your side a voice. I like it. This controversy may be bad for your company but it's great free publicity for your book. Especially if we publish excerpts in places like the *Silicon News,* where the venture capital folks will read them. Silicon Valley will eat this up. Just remember, Maxine, that once we get going, you'll need to produce more chapters, no matter how busy you are at Canopy. We can't leave your readers stranded."

"Oh, believe me, I know," said Maxine. "One chapter at a time. Even though Brendan is gone, there is plenty of material."

"Alright, then." Claudia raised her water bottle. "Here's to speaking ill of the dead. Not to mention writing ill of them."

Maxine and Gloria raise their water bottles too.

"May he rest in pieces," said Gloria.

Maxine looked at her friend. "Good line, Gloria. You should be a writer."

[18]
FAIL BETTER

 From the *Silicon News:*

> *Heard on the Road*: One of three founders of a certain East Bay agbio startup plans to publish a novel in which an aging scientist seduces three women scientists and steals their secrets... and takes those secrets to his grave.
>
> Sound familiar? When we said this was one for the books, we had no idea how right we were. Stay Tuned!

Joyce left her lab in frustration one day and went to see Rose. "No luck yet. The pup plants are still flowering and I don't know how much longer it will take. I'm going to meet with the head of Facilities at my old company and see if we can stay in this building longer."

"Great! I didn't know that was an option."

"It may not be. But I heard through the grapevine that there is a delay in their building plans. And if they're neither using this building nor tearing it down, why not let us stay a couple more months?"

"That would help a lot. Fingers crossed."

* * *

J oyce walked across the Sirona campus to the cluttered quarters of the Facilities Department. The broken fermenters in front of the director's office made her nostalgic for her time working with biologics. Rough benches were piled with dusty gadgets. The place reminded her of high school shop class. These guys might be working on million-dollar equipment but at heart they were just auto mechanics who got paid more.

Dennis Thompson was true to the breed. He was a burly grey-haired man in his fifties with the gruff manner of a guy who loves engines and puts up with people. His office was decorated with framed photographs of vintage airplanes. Two intricate model planes were suspended from the ceiling.

"Take a seat, Joyce. Good to see you."

"You too, Dennis. Thanks for meeting me."

"Yeah, glad for a break from all this paperwork." His desk was covered with proposals and binders for the city planning process.

"I'll bet. I hear there are permit delays on your expansion."

"That's right." Dennis sighed. "We are talking with the city, but it looks like a six-month setback. Could be more, but that's between you and me. We're just not where we want to be."

"Sorry to hear it. I know how hard you've worked."

"Yeah. Thanks. Anyway, what brings you over my way? Building working out OK?"

"Sure."

"But?"

"But... Canopy isn't where we want to be, either. Inventing can have delays, just like zoning. It would be great if we could stay a little longer at Sirona. Our timing and yours could work out really well. And—" This was Joyce's big selling point. "We would start paying rent. You're not likely to get somebody else to come in and pay for a six-month occupancy."

"I appreciate that, Joyce. I really do." Dennis did not sound excited.

"But?"

"Some of the stories going around about you and your friends are troubling."

"Like what?"

"Seducing some poor old guy and stealing his ideas, and then he dies suddenly... I even saw something about it in the newspaper."

Not this again. How frustrating. "That is not at all what happened."

"I'm sure it's not. I know you're not like that, Joyce. But these stories have made it all the way to corporate headquarters in Brussels, and upper management doesn't know you like we do."

"So, you're saying that Canopy has to be out of here at the end of the original twelve months? Even if you're not ready to tear down the building?"

"I'm saying more than that. I'm saying if you asked for more time, the higher ups in Brussels might make you move out now. My advice is to lay low. And start scoping out a new place. You folks have money?"

"Enough, for a while."

Dennis nodded. "Good. Make every penny count."

* * *

It was well past the dinner hour when the three founders of Canopy huddled around congealed pizza in the dim conference room. Everyone else had gone home and the only sound was the occasional flush of a distant toilet, the one rumored to be visited by ghosts.

"Thanks for trying to extend our stay, Joyce. Really. That showed great initiative." Maxine sounded impressed.

"Yeah, no problem. But all I got was a firm no. And I doubt that publishing the start of your novel will help with our landlords in Brussels."

Rose picked up a cold slice of dinner. "Joyce is right. Publishing your novel isn't exactly 'laying low.' It really sounds like we have to plan on a move, no matter what stage our development is in."

"But we do need to push back on the investor rumor mill." Maxine pulled the pepperoni off her slice.

"You're right, Max. It's a tough spot." Joyce stared at her paper plate. "Once our lab space is gone, we won't have the funds to start over."

"Publishing your story is a gamble," said Rose.

"Yes, I know. But it may be our only play."

"I thought we would have more results to show by now," said Joyce.

"We all were hoping," said Maxine. "But research takes time, that's all. We just need more time."

More time. They were already pushing it, working more hours than they were away. And it wasn't just the founders. The interns, now back in school, were still spending every hour they could at Canopy. Even Nash seemed to be there seven days a week. Something had to give.

* * *

Maxine closed the door to her office and made the phone call she had been putting off.

"Maxine! What a great surprise! How are you? I hear your new company is off with a bang."

"Yes, Benny, we are good. Working hard. And I bet you are too."

Ben Marks chuckled. "You know us. A laugh a minute in patent world. To what do I owe the pleasure?"

"I wanted to say hello and see how things were going, and also to check about my buyout. The money I put in to buy my partnership back in the day ought to come back to me right about now. And truth be told, I could use it. Or more accurately, Canopy could use it."

"Saving the planet is expensive, eh?"

"You have no idea."

"I'm sure. Your call is well timed, Maxine. The firm's quarterly partner's meeting was last week, and we reviewed your funding as part of our overall finances. I'm happy to report Stilton Ramsey will make installment payments to you beginning in about six months."

"Sorry, Ben, but I can't wait that long. We can only stay in Sirona space for a limited time, and I need money for new labs."

"Here's what we can do: We can write a letter confirming our intent to pay you back on a schedule."

"I can't get a lease with that."

"It's the best we can do. We have to pay our rent too."

"That isn't good enough."

"Maxine, you're a lawyer. Go review your partnership agreement. It gives our firm a lot of leeway about payback. Keep in mind you left us without much notice. We didn't have time to build a reserve to pay you back. We are trying our best to work with you. And like the saying goes, your lack of planning is not our emergency."

Maxine said goodbye, then crossed her arms and stared at nothing. Canopy was in danger and she was out of moves.

* * *

Pam sat with Gary on the front deck of her Berkeley Hills home, a modern box of glass and steel that clung to the hillside. Below them stood the white Tudor spires of the Claremont Hotel, with the San Francisco Bay beyond. After living there for decades, Pam still appreciated the view, but Gary was completely captivated. He loved sipping a glass of wine and gazing out through the palm trees that swayed in the breeze. And she loved watching his long-boned frame as he shaded his eyes against the setting sun.

"So, Joyce is talking about mortgaging your house and lending the money to Canopy?"

"Yes." Gary frowned. "With these rumors about stealing trade secrets, they are having trouble attracting investors. That damned Brendan may be dead but he's still causing trouble."

"Has she let her business partners know?"

"Not yet."

"Taking on debt is a big step. Do you want to do it?"

Gary turned to look at her. "Joyce loves that company. She was never this passionate about her career before. But frankly, I'm not keen. I'm not sure where Canopy is heading, and it seems risky. On the other hand, Joyce took a big risk for me when she agreed to open our marriage. I won't forget it."

"What is happening with Joyce and Gloria? I thought they were flirting."

"They were. I'm not sure that will go anywhere. But even before she met Gloria, Joyce was steadfast. She supported my relationship with you even when she didn't have someone else in her life."

"Well, I'm grateful she made the choice she did. And I can see why you want to help her with Canopy. If you decide to make the loan, you two could bunk here if things go awry."

Gary stood and took Pam's hand and led her inside, all the way to Pam's room, without saying a word. They stood face to face by her bed.

"What is this, Mr. Farrell?"

"This, Ms. Gregory, is both of us getting exactly what we want. We should all of us get what we most want." Gary cupped Pam's buttocks in his hands and pulled her to him so he could nuzzle the base of her neck.

"Ah. You do have a point," said Pam.

[19]
DEAD RECKONING

 From the *Silicon News*:

Heard on the Road: An established Bay Area publisher has approached us about serializing a salacious novel featuring three women scientists.

Should we take the bait? Surely not.

But can we resist? No way, San Jose.

Stay tuned...

Maxine's cell phone rang. The screen said it was Fred Hinkle. Should she take it? She sighed and then punched the button to put him on speaker.

"Hello, Fred."

"This is Dr. Fred Hinkle calling."

"Yes, what can I do for you?"

"You can stop slandering my deceased business partner. This plan to serialize your so-called 'novel' is despicable."

"Not to split hairs, but slander is speech. Writing is libel. Except in this case, writing is fiction, and thus is neither of those things."

"Yes, well, a lot of people believe that you are writing about

Brendan Burns. I intend to see you in court to stop you from defaming him, and I don't care what technical term you want to call it."

"Have you spoken with an attorney about this?"

"Not yet. I have calls out though. I'm not sitting on it."

"When you do hear back, what they're going to tell you is that you have no cause of action. Even if you were related to Burns, and even if you could prove that the writing was about him (which you can't, because it's fiction), but even then, no lawsuit could be brought."

"Why not?"

"Because dead people cannot sue for libel. The dead don't worry about their reputations. Full stop."

"I won't believe this until I hear it from a neutral attorney."

"Suit yourself. Or look it up online. We're talking first year law school material."

"Even if that is true, I'll still see you in court for stealing our trade secrets."

Maxine held her head in her hands. "You are wrong about that too, Fred. And the sooner you see it the better."

* * *

On the day the first chapter of Maxine's book appeared in the *Silicon News*, her phone rang off the hook. There were crank calls from men with propositions, some of which were formal, and some not so formal. Other calls were from reporters wanting the lowdown on where the story originated. By nine in the morning Maxine stopped answering the phone, and only made an exception when Gordon's number came up on her screen.

"Hello Max. Say, the start of your book is a real eye-opener, and a fun read. Certainly a different perspective on the rumors that have been floating around—if that was your intent. A much more sympathetic perspective."

"No comment, Mr. Hendricks."

He laughed. "I didn't expect you to spill those beans. But I have to say, if you think Canopy is going to fly, I'm more inclined to take your word. And I can tell you that my business partners feel the same way."

"Thank you, Gordon, I really appreciate that. But there's no need to take my word for anything. We're developing good data. Once we file the patent on the full invention, I can bring my team to show you."

"Alright. That sounds great. And your plan is to go public?"

"Yes, as soon as we have initial units from our pilot plant, with high efficiency CO_2 conversion and photovoltaic activity."

"I hope you get there. You've always been ambitious, Maxine. But this takes the cake. Saving the world, one rooftop at a time."

"The world could use saving."

"You're right about that." Gordon paused. "It will be good to see you, my friend. I'd really like to get together and talk about things other than work."

It was Maxine's turn to pause. "I'm pretty busy these days—"

"I can't even imagine. How you're writing a book while running Canopy is beyond me."

"--and I don't get involved with business partners. But after we go public and your firm is paid out—"

"Yes. After that, let's spend some time together and see how it goes. Would you like that?"

"I look forward to it."

"As do I."

* * *

Claudia, Maxine and Gloria met for dinner on the night the first chapter of Maxine's serial novel was published. Claudia, who had an old-fashioned appreciation of a physical newspaper, read a review aloud from a printed copy. "Let's see what they have to say. Here it is: 'Ms. Vargas' first chapter appears to be a veiled report of her brief affair with the late Brendan Burns, a would-be inventor who died suddenly in October—rumor has it, just after all three founders of Canopy Enterprises ended their associations with him.'" She put down the newspaper.

"Good grief, it's practically an accusation; the police will be here any minute."

Gloria grimaced. "Who said there's no such thing as bad publicity?"

Claudia nodded and continued. "Hmm... 'Her language is so delightful, and the circumstance so wicked, that we cannot wait to read the next chapter and find out whether Vargas can put certain rumors to bed.' As it were. Well, if that doesn't get you phone calls, Maxine, I don't know what will. From investors, I mean, not threats of a libel suit."

"I've been getting calls of all kinds. Remember when Fred Hinkle complained I was maligning his friend? Just the other day I had the privilege of telling him the dead can't sue for libel. Nor can their estates."

Claudia put down the paper. "Really? Why not?"

Gloria explained. "Because there are no damages. Dead people don't care about their reputations."

"They might well care. How do you know?" Claudia warmed to her subject. "Have you ever been to a séance? No? How do you know what concerns the dead?"

Gloria and Maxine look at each other.

"That's a good point, actually. But not a question the law can answer." Maxine shrugged.

"Science can't tell us that either. Sorry," said Gloria.

* * *

The next morning, Marisol stopped Rose in the hall. "Isis says that back when you were a professor, the three of you were dating the same guy, and you discovered it and told Joyce and Maxine. And that's what Maxine's book is really about. Is that true?"

Rose smiled at the worried intern. "Marisol, remember when we talked about how life doesn't stop at forty? Or even sixty?"

"Yes."

"And if life doesn't stop, we don't stop making mistakes, either. And if we keep making mistakes, some of them turn out to be good."

"I remember all that, Rose. But you haven't answered my question. Is Maxine's book really a true story?"

"She says it's fiction. I'll have to trust her on that."

"Are you going to read it?"

"No." Rose winked. "I already know what it says."

* * *

After work that day, Maxine and Nash stood in Nash's back yard, looking up at the array on his roof.

"Not a flower to be seen," said Nash.

"Joyce turned off the expression of a growth hormone. She thinks they have that flowering problem licked. Of course, they've been playing whack-a-mole with lots of problems. We'll see."

"Meanwhile have you thought about how you're going to collect the electricity?"

"Some. We have the ammeter set up for now."

"Yes but you'll need something better. Something like the opposite of a wireless phone charger. On an array like a wire mesh, not that thick metal tray you're using now. You want the whole thing as light as possible, right?"

Maxine looked impressed. "Nash, if you could design something like that—I mean, I'd like to do it but I don't have the bandwidth. Do you?"

"Let me cobble something together."

"I bet you know this kind of thing like the back of your hand."

"Sure. Go down the arm, turn left at the thumb."

Maxine laughed. "Terrific. Thanks Nash. You'll have your name on a Canopy patent."

Nash shook his head. "Don't worry about that. You women are the brains. I'm just the handyman for this outfit."

* * *

When the third chapter of her novel published, Maxine received another call from Gordon.

"You've turned quite a few heads with your book chapters."

"Is that a good thing?"

"I'd say so. A month ago there was a lot of skepticism about Canopy around Silicon Valley. The narrative was three women preying on an old man. Some people even thought you might have had something to do with his death. But all that turned on a dime. You could even say a paradigm, if you didn't mind the play on words."

"Oh please, not that murder conspiracy nonsense. We weren't there when Brendan died, and I'm not sure how anybody could make someone choke to death by remote control. Although judging by his funeral, certain women might have enjoyed it. But I'm glad to hear the book is changing people's views, even though my novel is complete fiction."

"Of course it is, Max. One hundred percent invention."

[20]
A BRIDGE TOO FAR

Joyce and Rose were slumped at a table near the tanks in their lab, trying to come up with ideas to solve their newest problem: that their prize plants, that did so well at photosynthesizing and making electricity, turned out to have no tolerance for bright sunlight.

"We are so close," Joyce moaned.

"We are so tired," Rose whispered.

"Ok. Let's get it together. We gotta cross the finish line. Close is only good in horseshoes."

"Joyce, how many random clichés can you string together?"

"Just you wait. I'm still getting warmed up."

Rose sat up straight. "That kind of torture is pretty motivating. Alright. Let's review our options. First, we could graft in genes from plants that close up their pores when the light is too bright. Some desert plants do that."

"That's a thought. I have reservations, but I'll hold off. We're in brainstorming mode."

"Thank you. I appreciate that. Second, we could graft in genes to turn our plants maroon. You've seen plants like that. The dark coloring helps them withstand bright sun."

"Good. Another thought. I have the same objection, which I will once again reserve."

"Keep reserving, Joyce. Third option: We could figure out why the heck our darling little plants are behaving like this in the first place and undo whatever we did that caused it."

"The direct approach. I like it. Anything else?"

"Nope, that's what I've got. How about you, Joyce? Any ideas?"

"I'm a chemist. I don't have ideas about biological systems. I just see problems."

"Alright, let's go with that. What problems do you see with these ideas?"

"Your first two ideas, closing the pores and turning the plants purple, have the same flaw: they're trying to do brain surgery with a sledgehammer. If you do either of those things, you're basically counteracting everything we've done to make our plants more efficient at photosynthesis."

"Yes, I can see that. Although if we had the time, we might be able to fine tune either solution. And what's your problem with the third idea?"

"The challenge there is time. You are right that all three of them share that problem, but this one most of all. Looking for the source of the bright light issue would be way worse than looking for a needle in a haystack. We've messed with the genome so much that teasing out which change or combination of changes caused this problem would take months. And we don't have months."

"No, we don't. You're absolutely right. We got into this mess in a hurry and we need to get back out of it in a hurry. So what do we do now?"

Joyce shook her head. "I am fresh out of ideas. And now we have to prep for a trial? I'm beginning to think we're done."

. . .

Because despite Maxine's assurances that there would be no trial, the day was upon them. Gloria called together the founders and reassured them, "Remember that Fred has no basis for this suit. Hinkle's lawyer is a publicity hound. Weston will try to discredit your backgrounds before he presents whatever flimsy story they've concocted about how you stole Brendan's ideas. He must be hoping we'll cave and make him an offer before the case is thrown out."

Maxine shrugged. "What would we offer? Canopy has no assets."

Gloria looked grim. "Our patent applications. Our future patents. But we are not going to do it."

"We're not going to do much, from what I can tell," said Joyce. "We've hit a wall in our research, and this lawsuit is sapping what little energy we have left. It feels like a bridge too far."

"Hang in there, team," said Maxine. "Let's see how this week goes."

[21]
THE TRIAL

There they were in the courtroom, at the defendants' table, wearing their best suits: Maxine, Joyce and Rose, with Gloria defending them. It was a Silicon Valley media fest. Both the legal reporter and the scandal reporter from the *Silicon News* were at the front of the pack.

At the plaintiff's table, Fred Hinkle somehow managed to look both aggrieved and deflated. By contrast, his young lawyer had the pent-up energy of an overwound top.

Judge Gina Fry walked in and bid them all be seated. James Weston stood. "Your Honor, we call Dr. Rose Bingham to the stand."

Gloria patted her arm. Rose could feel her heart beating wildly as she approached the witness chair. Silly, she told herself. Nothing to defend. They had invented the Canopy, not Brendan.

"Dr. Bingham, could you please summarize your educational background for the court?"

"I have a Bachelors degree in physiology from UCLA and a Ph.D. in cell biology from Stanford. I retired last year as a full professor at UC Berkeley."

"And in your undergraduate program, how many courses did you take in botany?"

"Many of the classes I took touched on the cellular structure and physiology of plants. I—"

"Please answer the question, Dr. Bingham. Would a copy of your college record refresh your memory?" Weston brandished a sheet of paper.

"That won't be necessary. I took one botany course."

"Just one. And your Ph.D. program—was that focused on plant life?"

"My dissertation was on cellular evolution."

"Evolution of plant cells? Or animal cells?"

"Animal cells. Dinosaur cells."

"Now, I have here a chronological list of your publications over the past five years. I've drawn a red line to separate your publications before and after the death of Brendan Burns. Please tell the court how many publications on botany appear above the red line."

"There are none."

"And how many botany papers are listed after the date of his death?"

"Seven."

"Out of a total of?"

"Seven."

"And did Dr. Burns teach you what you know about botany?"

"Objection." That was from Gloria. "Leading the witness."

"Withdrawn." Fred's attorney stifled a smile. "Let me rephrase: How and when did you learn the intricacies of plant science necessary to the Canopy invention?"

"I learned by reading and experimentation, just like anyone else who makes an invention. And by working with my colleague Dr. Joyce Farrell."

"Yes, we'll hear from Dr. Farrell next about her background in plant science, or lack of it. But as for you, Dr. Bingham, do you expect this court to believe that a dinosaur specialist suddenly transformed herself into a botanist, with no help from the late Dr. Burns, who was known as an innovator in this field?"

"Objection, Your Honor. Asked and answered."

"Sustained."

"Thank you, Your Honor." Weston smiled. "Dr. Bingham, isn't it true that in fact you used Dr. Burns' concepts and innovations as the basis for what you call your product at Canopy, without giving credit to Dr. Burns or his surviving partner, Dr. Hinkle?"

"No, that's—"

Gloria stood. "Objection, Your Honor. The attorney is testifying. And badgering the witness."

"Sustained."

"No further questions." Hinkle's lawyer had made his point. "Dr. Bingham, you may step down."

The judge hit her gavel. "This court has other business in the afternoon and tomorrow morning. This case will reconvene at one P.M. tomorrow."

* * *

That afternoon, after Rose's debacle, Joyce had no energy for the lab. She wanted nothing more than to curl up at home. Gary was out for the evening, which was fine, because Joyce did not want to talk with anyone. She wrapped herself in a quilt, turned off the ringer on her phone, and lay down on the couch. But when Dennis' name came up on her phone, she decided to take the call.

"Hi Joyce. Are you on deck tomorrow?"

"Yes, I'm afraid so. Are people talking about today's testimony?"

"Not just people. Sirona brass. If this thing doesn't turn around, they're going to turn off the utilities to your building and tell you to leave early."

"Holy hell, Dennis. No pressure though."

"Just thought you should know, Joyce."

"Thanks. I think."

Maxine also went straight home after court. She was not one for strong spirits, but she made an exception and was sitting poolside with a gin and tonic when Gordon called.

"Maxine."

"Yes, Gordon. You heard about today."

"I heard. And Joyce is up tomorrow?"

"Yes."

"Do you think she'll do any better on the stand?"

"It's unlikely. Her publication history is a lot like Rose's."

"Well, I have to tell you that so far, this trial is blowing a hole through your chances of financing. Certainly with Tarth, and probably with anyone else. Sorry, Max." Gordon could hear ice cubes clinking at the other end of the line as Maxine shook her glass nervously.

"What are you drinking?"

"Gin and tonic. But I may switch to straight gin."

* * *

The next morning, Fred Hinkle stopped at the college before heading over to the Oakland courthouse. A young man stood at his office door.

"Come in, come in." The tiny, windowless space was crammed with books and papers. Fred cleared books off a chair and gestured. "Here, sit."

"Thanks."

"What can I do for you? Are you a student at our community college?"

Jake shook his head. "No. My name is Jake Bennett. I'm at Cal."

"And what do you study?"

"Engineering and Computer Science."

"Good man. To what do I owe the pleasure?"

"I work part time at a used electronics store down on University Avenue. Redford's."

"I know the place. Go on."

"A while back a guy came in with a DVD carousel to sell. Didn't say where he got it."

Jake shifted in his chair and folded his arms. Fred looked at him. "What's the problem? Do you think he stole it?"

"No, I don't. I think he's with one of these outfits that cleans out places where people have died."

"What makes you think that?"

"He was wearing a uniform with some company name that sounded like that. A bunch of DVDs were still in the carousel. I didn't want them; made the guy take them away and get rid of them. But one of the DVDs was a bootleg *Star Trek* DVD and I kept that one, just for fun."

"Alright, I'll bite. What was really on the disc? Not *Star Trek*, I assume."

"No. Not *Star Trek*. I've read in the *Silicon News* about your lawsuit against the women at Canopy, and about your business partner who died."

"May I assume there's a point here somewhere?"

"Yeah." Jake put a silver disc on the desk. "This DVD is a sex tape of Brendan Burns and one of the women you're suing. I saw pictures of both of them in the paper. The DVD carousel must have been cleaned out of the Burn's house."

Fred leaned forward. "And I suppose you want to give me this disc. For a price."

"That's right. I figure you could use it in your case."

"I'm no lawyer, Jake, but I'm pretty sure something like that is not admissible."

Jake shrugged. "Don't most of these cases settle?"

"Yes, that's my understanding. But what you are suggesting is tantamount to blackmail."

Jake nodded. "Isn't that basically what you're doing? Shaking down these women?"

Fred's face reddened. "Absolutely not! I am standing up for my deceased business partner."

"Whatever you say. Do you want the disc or not?"

Fred opened a drawer and took out a checkbook. "How many copies are there?"

"Just the one. I sure don't want it. Old people sex." Jake shuddered.

"Perhaps you don't realize that youth is temporary. But back to business. Did you upload this anywhere?"

"No. The quality is pretty bad. I don't think anyone would be interested, except the woman involved."

Fred wrote out a check and held it out toward Jake but did not put it in his outstretched fingers. "Half of this amount is payment for the disc. The other half is to pay for your absolute silence. You may not think it, since I teach at the less stellar institute of higher learning in Palo Alto, but people in our industry listen to me. If you speak a word about this disc, if I even read a rumor about it in the paper, you will have one hell of a time getting a job in the Valley. I can make that happen. Understood?"

"Yes. I understand."

"Good. Now off with you."

* * *

That afternoon in court, Rose was hoping that Joyce would fare better than she had. After all, Joyce was a cool cucumber. But it was the same litany: How many botany courses as an undergraduate? None. Graduate work in plant science? None. Journal publications on botany? None—until a flurry after Brendan's death.

Rose glanced across the room and noticed that Fred Hinkle was sitting with his face in his hands. He looked as dejected as Rose felt in that moment. She wondered why.

Then it was Maxine's turn, and the questioning shifted. How could she submit a patent on a stolen invention? Didn't that violate her professional ethics?

"I know my work and I know my company's work. It is the highest caliber. Original ideas, well executed, based on reliable data generated by Canopy. I'm sure Dr. Hinkle is a fine scientist, but this is not his invention, nor is it his deceased partner's invention. The photovoltaic solar panel is a Canopy invention. Full stop."

Joyce leaned over to Rose's ear. "Damn. We always knew she was good. But she is really good."

Ah, but was it enough?

Tomorrow Fred Hinkle would have his say.

* * *

That night was the first time in a long time that Rose, Joyce and Maxine had visited The Lab. This time they were not festive, and they were also not alone: Nash and Gloria were there to support them. Everybody was drinking beer.

"Beer may be all we can afford." Joyce was only half joking.

"I don't understand why Hinkle is so intent on getting control of our company." Rose stared into her beer mug. "It's not like it's worth anything, if the patents get thrown out."

Maxine looked around the table and saw nothing but downcast faces. "Let's not get ahead of ourselves. It's clear that Fred Hinkle sees the value of our invention, or he would not fight so hard. And we don't know what he's planning to say on the stand. We do know the truth: that we didn't take ideas from either him or Brendan. But how far they got on their own, how closely their ideas parallel ours, we just have no idea. For all we know, they may not have much at all."

"However it goes tomorrow," Rose said, "we have one another. All of us. We are smart and energetic and —"

"And old, don't forget old." Nash was sitting next to Rose and squeezed her hand under the table.

Rose laughed. "Thanks a lot. But we have tons of energy and lots of ideas. If we lose, we'll do something else, something that has nothing to do with botany. Maybe a substitute for Mace that only knocks out men." At this, Nash stood up halfway like he was going to run from the room, and Rose pulled him down by the back of his shirt. "Or maybe—who knows?—an interstellar drive that runs on starlight. Don't give up, let's none of us give up. The possibilities are endless."

Joyce looked skeptical. "The possibilities may be endless, Rose, but the money is not. Sure, men whose companies go belly up just go somewhere else with a pat on the back for trying. But the stats on women whose companies fail are totally different. 'Who are they, to think they could do something grand? Why aren't they acting like good worker bees?' That's the message we get, when a woman-run business fails."

Maxine put her hand on Joyce's arm. "Alright, Joyce, nobody is saying that Canopy is going to fail. The results are not in. Let's see what happens tomorrow."

"Here, here. Worry is the only thing that's improved by procrastinating." Nash raised his mug. "Cheers, everybody."

"Cheers," the women answered. But none of them looked cheerful.

* * *

N ash drove Rose home from The Lab. By the time they arrived, it was only eight hours before they were due in court for the last day of testimony. Rose looked the worse for wear.

"You don't do well with alcohol, do you? How many beers did you drink?"

"Three." Rose held her head in her hands as they pulled into Maxine's driveway. Nash opened the passenger door and put his arm around Rose as they walked back to the cottage.

"That's more than usual, isn't it?"

"Two more than usual. But tonight is unusual."

Nash took her key and opened Rose's front door. "What can I do to help?"

Rose sat down heavily on her couch. "Thanks, Nash, for listening to me blather on about the lawsuit. You already do so much."

He sat down beside her. "Not really. I do a bit, here and there. One little thing I have done is blocked deposits from Canopy to my bank account."

"Why?"

"I don't want to be a kept man."

"What do you mean? You work just as hard as the rest of us. Your work is stellar."

"Why, thank you, Ma'am."

"I mean it. And I don't want you to run short of cash because we're struggling."

"Not bloody likely." Nash shook his head. "How many old IT guys do you see under bridges? I helped design Linux, back in the day."

"What is Linux?"

"You are supposed to be impressed, woman!" Nash took her hand between his warm hands. "The point is, I'm fine. And I could do more. Maybe it's my turn to sell an overpriced house. Want a roommate?"

Rose put her arms around him. "You lovely man. We said we would take it slow and we should stick to that—no matter what's happening at Canopy. But it's wonderful of you to offer."

He tickled her ribs. "Just what is it you think I'm offering? Hmm? Come over here and find out."

"Oh!"

"You like that? There's more where that came from."

Perhaps she was not so exhausted after all.

N ash took Rose's hand and led her into the oak paneled bedroom. Under the arched ceiling, her queen-sized bed looked cozy and warm, covered in a blue and purple geometric quilt. "You're a star, whatever happens tomorrow." He undid her top button. "I only consort with geniuses, you know."

Rose laughed and snuggled up to him. "Then you should go see Joyce. She's the real brains at Canopy."

"I don't want to be with Joyce. I want to be with you." He kept undoing her buttons and slid her blouse down, then leaned in to kiss her shoulders.

She shivered. "Let's get under the covers, shall we?"

"Alright. But I want to see you. Every inch of you."

They took off each other's clothes then, as shy and excited as if it were their first time with anyone. As he removed each item, every time he brushed his fingers across her skin, Rose trembled with excitement. He continued to kiss, first her neck, then her shoulders, then her breasts, while he held her buttocks in his strong hands. The sensation was electric. She twined her fingers in his hair, drew him even closer. He pulled down her slacks and then slid his face down to her belly. Parting her thighs, he kissed his way down until she gasped as his lips found what they had been seeking, and his tongue followed. Her body reached up to meet him until, sated, she lay back. And then he, inflamed by the sounds of her desire, lay his naked body over her and came into her, and she found that she was ready with all her being to be filled with his passion. They slept and woke and made love again, this time slowly and gently, so that she felt like a boat at anchor, at peace and moving on the water. When she reached her peak with him inside her, while he kissed her mouth as if it were a sacred act, she felt the sensation of making love with the universe itself.

As they snuggled together in the dark afterwards and began to fall asleep again, he kissed her shoulder and said, "Will you still talk with me when you're rich and famous?"

Rose smiled. "I'll consider it."

In the morning, Rose floated out to the kitchen and found Nash making breakfast.

She hugged him from the back as he worked. "Why are you doing that? I should be making you breakfast."

"Somebody likes to sleep in, so somebody else cooked."

"Sleep in? It's six in the morning. Practically the middle of the night."

"Practically noon, you mean." He carried two plates out to the table, which was already set. A pot of tea brewed on a placemat in the middle of the table.

"I do like this house," he said as they sat down. "Nice proportions, well built. A bit like the woman across the table."

"Oh, this breakfast is delicious, Nash. Yes, the house is great. I even have my own flower bed, out back."

He looked at her over the edge of his teacup. "But you have more gardening to do."

"What do you mean?" She bit an English muffin, toasted just right.

"I got a good lashing last night." Nash mimed going through a jungle, face first. "Now I know what they really mean by pussy whipped."

Rose turned bright red. "You are impossible, you know that don't you?"

He looked at her, all wide-eyed innocence. "Me? I have no idea what you mean."

There was a knock on the door and Maxine opened it and peeked in. "Rose, I— Oh, good morning, Nash." Maxine raised her eyebrows.

"Good morning, Maxine."

Maxine continued. "I was just going to tell you, Rose, not to go for a swim this morning. The pump is out. I'll call someone later."

"Let me take a look before I head for the office." Nash took a last swallow of tea. He rose from the table, his dishes in hand, then leaned over to kiss Rose. "Bye, Babe. Good luck today."

He dropped his dishes in the sink and passed Maxine on his way out of the house. "Bye, Boss. Good luck to you, too."

Maxine walked over to Rose. "Well! I guess he fixes all kinds of things."

Rose shook her head. "Oh, now, don't you start."

"Took your mind off the trial, didn't he?"

"Yes he did. For a while."

* * *

The night before he was scheduled to testify, Fred Hinkle was alone at home when he finally slid the bootleg DVD into the player in his living room. He had read Brendan's autopsy report and knew that his friend had choked on popcorn at home. The Popcorn Palace, as Brendan called his house. Fred also knew that Brendan loved watching movies, even when he was alone. And if this was the kind of movie Jake claimed it was, Brendan could easily have been distracted enough to aspirate his buttery snack.

But that was just conjecture. Fred was only putting off the inevitable. Time to watch the damned thing, before his wife came home and he had to explain. He pushed the button.

His first impression was a jumble of flesh on a bed, mostly Brendan's massive bulk. And in a moment, Brendan turned his head and leered at the camera. The woman with him seemed totally unconscious of the filming, was oblivious to anything but being with Brendan. And the smirk on Brendan's face told it all. That was Brendan grinning at his future self, celebrating that he had put one over on the naked woman in his bed. And the woman was Rose Bingham, whom Fred had seen in the witness stand just the day before. The look of adoration on her face was meant only for Brendan. Fred was ashamed to witness it.

The conclusion was unmistakable: This was no consensual filming. This was an illicit movie, made by a man totally without decency. He had seen enough. Fred hit the stop button. But instead of stopping, the disc skipped ahead. Now Rose and Brendan were lying quietly with the covers up, talking.

"If you were trying to improve on photosynthesis, which plants would be your first candidates to modify? Algae? Plankton? Or something else?"

"Why all the questions about photosynthesis, Brendan?"

"You enjoy chatting about biology. My job is to keep you amused, in every possible way." Brendan lifted Rose's hand and sucked on her index finger. "Hmm? Which species?"

This time Fred hit the eject button, his face red with anger. Brendan had betrayed these women, had exploited their bodies and minds. And Fred himself had been played. He had been so taken in that he was still acting on Brendan's lies, even after his death. Fred picked up the disc between his thumb and forefinger, touching it as little as possible, as if it were a soiled diaper. Then he walked into his study and pushed the start button on his paper shredder. The disc made a satisfying grinding sound as it was destroyed.

[22]
TRIAL'S END

 From the *Silicon News*:

Heard on the Road: In advance of serializing a certain rather inflammatory novel, our fine establishment received some rather pointed notes from a fresh-faced local lawyer. While we are always glad to hear from our readers, at times we must refresh their memories about the First Amendment. To the Constitution. Heard of it? Consider yourself reminded, Mr. Attorney.

And as for the rest of you: Stay tuned...

The courtroom was full of reporters on the final day of the trial. There were conversations all over the room, journalists huddling with scientists, trying for an advance read on the day. At exactly nine o'clock, Judge Fry entered the room and everyone stood. "Come to order," she said. "You may be seated. Plaintiff's counsel, please call your witness."

Jim Weston stood tall. "Thank you, Your Honor. Dr. Fred Hinkle, please take the stand."

Fred Hinkle made his way to the front of the room, pausing to glance at the founders of Canopy, his face unreadable. His attorney spoke.

"Dr. Hinkle, we appreciate your being here today. It must be difficult to confront this challenge when the death of Dr. Burns, your friend and research partner, is still relatively recent. Counsel for Canopy Enterprises has agreed to stipulate to your qualifications as a botanist, and so I begin by asking you: In your expert opinion, how realistic is the claim that the three women who founded this company, none of whom had more than a passing familiarity with plant science, were the true inventors of the photovoltaic solar panel?"

Fred stared at his lawyer for a moment, emotions at play on his features. Then he seemed to collect his thoughts. "Actually, it's quite realistic, given the culture at Canopy."

A low murmur came from the audience in the courtroom. Dr. Hinkle's lawyer cleared his throat. "Perhaps I should clarify—"

"Not necessary, thanks. From what I have seen of Canopy's publications, they are doing several key things very well. For one, they must be working damned hard. They do a tremendous number of experiments. Edison once said that the measure of success is how many experiments you can fit in a day, and these women have generated terrific output in the short time they have been together. Another essential element of invention is pulling ideas from multiple sources. The genetically engineered plants in the Canopy solar panel show the highest order of innovative thought. Making electricity with plants that are simultaneously putting out a supercharged level of oxygen and binding huge amounts of carbon dioxide? Golly. I'm sure there will still be challenges, but the Canopy system is a fantastic invention. A wise man once said that specialization is for insects. No, these women are not specialists in botany. They are the founders of an idea powerhouse."

The room went so wild that the court reporter could barely hear the witness' last words. And she strained to hear when Gloria rose and moved to dismiss the case. Judge Fry hit the gavel. "Motion granted. Case dismissed."

* * *

F red Hinkle stood on the courthouse steps with Rose, Maxine and Joyce. "I owe you and everyone at your company an apology," he said. "How did it take me so long to see it? The women at Brendan's memorial made clear what manner of man he was. And the three of you told me often enough. I listened to him and ignored all of you. I come from a generation that was taught to hear what men say and ignore what women say. But that's no excuse. Ignoring data is unscientific. Ignoring you was shameful."

Maxine shook Fred's hand. "Thank you for admitting your mistake. That took courage."

Fred shook his head. "But it's a bit late. I've taken energy away from your real work, your important work."

Maxine nodded. "This has been tough on us, but then we are tough, and we'll get through it. Will you tell us one thing, though?"

"If I can."

"Who finally convinced you that we invented the Canopy system?"

"Brendan did. He paid a visit from beyond the grave and told the truth at last."

The three women glanced at each other, baffled. Maxine spoke up. "I don't suppose you're going to explain?"

"Not one word. Best wishes to you and your company. Farewell." Fred turned and walked away, waving off reporters as he went.

Rose looked after his receding figure. "Are you sure we shouldn't offer him a job?"

"No," said Maxine and Joyce, almost in unison.

* * *

P am and Gary were having an early drink on the terrace at the Claremont Hotel.

"If Joyce needs comforting after the trial, you should go to her."

"Thank you, Pam, I—" Gary's cell phone rang. "It's her."

Gary answered and put the phone to his ear. "He said what? Are you kidding? Congratulations, Hon! You'll be hearing from the financiers now! Sure, I know, another hurdle on the prototype, but so close... yes, I love you too! OK, talk later!"

Pam smiled. "I take it things went well?"

"Fred Hinkle has completely recanted. The case is dismissed."

"Terrific! I guess you'll cancel that mortgage application now."

"Yes, once they finish their prototype."

"I was going to tell you to pull the plug on it, even if the trial went badly."

"Why?"

"Unlike Brendan, I really am sitting on a pile of cash. And I can't think of anything I'd rather do than invest in a company that's trying to save the planet."

Gary took her hands in his. "You're a good woman, Pam."

She smiled at him. "Thanks. It's easy to be good when you're happy."

* * *

W hen she was not busy running Canopy Enterprises, Maxine spent her time in the lab where she developed materials for Canopy solar panels. In truth, it was a much bigger job than she had time for. Last summer she had not even had time to line up her own interns, so she was happy and relieved when Isis volunteered to transfer to the solar panel lab.

"Thanks for helping out, Isis. I'm surrounded by biologists and chemists, and we really need engineering students like you. We are testing a variety of materials for the panels of our roof systems. And then we'll need to build prototypes of the full systems."

"It's great to be here. I'm glad Marisol told me you needed a hand. She and I were both in Dr. Bingham's biology class at Cal last year."

"Yes, Rose told me."

Just then Rose came into the room. "Hello Isis, Maxine. Isis, I'm happy you made it over here. Listen, I'm glad I caught both of you. We're still working on the problem that stymied us before the trial. Our modified plants generate a ton of oxygen and bind a whole lot of carbon dioxide, which is great. Plus they make electricity at a terrific rate. The problem is, when we expose them to really bright sunlight, they can't function. In fact, it kills them."

Maxine shook her head. "No genetic magic to fix that problem?"

"No." Rose frowned. "We've tried so many things, and no progress."

Isis spoke up. "What if we used solar panel material that darkens when the light is too bright?"

Maxine turned to Isis. "Good thought. But wouldn't that just undo what we're trying to do?"

"Not if we used solar panel material that generates electricity when it darkens. We don't have to invent that, it's already on the market. We studied that stuff in Materials Science class last semester."

Rose looked excited. "So our plants would make oxygen and electricity at all levels of light, and when it was too sunny, the panels would shield the plants and make extra electricity."

"Exactly." Isis beamed.

Rose nodded. "These panels would meet our goal of cleaning the air and giving us renewable energy."

Maxine grinned. "What a great idea, Isis. Let's work up prototypes with different sensitivities and see where this goes."

Joyce walked into the lab. "What's going on? I could hear the three of you from the hallway."

"I think we've got it, Joyce." Maxine clapped Isis on the shoulder. "Thanks to our great intern here. We'll need to refine it but I think we've found a solution to our problem with sunny days that still meets our specs for electrical output. The answer is in the structural material."

[23]
THE DOG AND PONY SHOW

From the *Silicon News*:

Heard on the Road: At long last, investors are lining up to fund Canopy Enterprises, an East Bay agbio startup founded by a biology professor from Cal, a former VP of Sirona Pharmaceuticals, and a retired partner from the top patent firm of Stilton Ramsey.

Why the long wait? Company president Maxine Vargas (the author of *Brilliant Charming Bastard*) just smiles and says: "Timing is everything."

As described in its patent application, the full prototype of the Canopy Roof System was a rectangle about three feet by four feet. The wire mesh across the bottom that held the modified plants also extended up the sides, allowing air to pass through while protecting the plants. At the top, the mesh met the special plastic that darkened in the brightest sunlight and generated electricity.

When the first two prototypes were finished and tested, Maxine called everyone to see them in the engineering lab. "Let's turn out the lights," said Maxine, and the group stood there in darkness. "Everything we worked and sacrificed for is right here in this room, and the most precious part is the power we found in each other. Thank you all, for everything. Now let's switch the lights back on and Isis, please hold up the ammeter. We're indoors, so the results are nothing like we'll see on a rooftop, but still..."

Isis held up the meter so all could see the reading.

"...still damned impressive. Ten times the power per square inch of our nearest competitor. Not to mention, we're cleaning the air as we go. Tomorrow we'll issue our press release. And next week we'll take a prototype down to Sand Hill Road to show our investors at Tarth Capital. Nothing does the trick like show and tell. We could send them a thousand pages of test results and it wouldn't have the impact of a good dog and pony show. So let's make it a great one."

When Maxine finished, Nash walked over to her. "You're absolutely right. People believe what they experience much more than what they read."

"Yeah. I haven't worked out how we will get a roof panel down there, though."

"We could strap it to the roof of a car, or a van. In fact, I have an idea." Nash began scribbling on a piece of paper. "Remind me the exact dimensions and weight of one panel, and how much energy output. And promise me you'll go down there on a sunny day."

"Sure. Why?"

"You'll see."

For the next few days, Rose was closeted with the other founders, practicing presentations, putting the finishing touches on their slides. Meanwhile Nash was intent on his project, ensconced in the mancave garage at his house. When he finished, Nash came by Canopy and asked Maxine if he could borrow one of the two prototypes the company had built.

"What are you up to?"

"I'm onto something. Trust me. You will like it."

"I do trust you, Nash. Go for it."

. . .

The next day, not ten minutes after the Canopy press release about the successful prototypes, Maxine received a call from her former partner, Ben Marks.

"Maxine, it's been a while."

"Yes it has, Ben. What can I do for you?

Ben laughed. "Actually, it's time I did something for you. Good news, Maxine: We've put together your partnership buyout and we're about to send you a check for the full amount. Sorry it took so long."

"That's very good news. As you've probably heard, we'll present our prototype at Tarth Capital next week. I expect an excellent outcome on funding. But I'll put that partnership money to good use on another project."

"I'd love to know what that project is."

"All in good time, Ben. I'm not telling yet."

Her ex-partner laughed. "You are full of surprises, Max. I am sorry we were not able to send you the funds a few months ago."

Sure, thought Maxine, *I'll bet you're sorry, now that we're on top, and you'd like to represent us.* Aloud she said, "It's the Law of Money, Ben. A check shows up at the moment you least need it."

"Indeed. Well. Gloria has been generous to spend her sabbatical with you when she could have been in Tahiti. When she comes back to us, just know that whatever Stilton Ramsey can do to support Canopy's intellectual property needs going forward, we are here for you."

"Duly noted. And thanks for sending the funds you owe me."

Maxine hung up. Her next call was to Gloria. "Hi there. How would you like a job?"

Gloria laughed. "I have a job. At that place where you used to work."

"I know. How would you like a better job?"

"I'm listening," said Gloria.

* * *

Later that day, Gloria stopped by Joyce's office and told her the news.

"So you see, Joyce, I'd love to be General Counsel at Canopy."

"Congratulations on the offer! Have you accepted?"

Gloria shook her head. "The problem is, I'm still holding out hope that you and I will get together. And I never date a colleague."

"What about our date last summer?"

"I was on sabbatical from my law firm, so technically you and I weren't colleagues. And now I'm scheduled to go back to the firm. I'm still a partner, though it's been a while since I stopped by. I don't want to put you on the spot, it's just that I won't take this offer from Maxine if there's any chance for you and me. But you may not be interested, or you may still be processing your breakup with Brendan—"

Joyce put a finger to Gloria's lip. "I get it. I'm amazed you would think of basing your career plans on me. But if you want to come join Canopy, maybe you could bend your rules a little?"

"Anything is possible."

"I haven't been avoiding you. I've just been consumed with this invention. How about I call Gary and tell him I'll be late tonight."

Gloria smiled. "Didn't we do that once before?"

"We did. At your house; should I call from there again?"

Joyce was more than late; she never went home at all. As the sun rose the next morning she was warm in Gloria's arms. Gloria was asleep behind her, and Joyce felt the generous softness of Gloria's breasts against her back. In her sleep, Gloria was cupping Joyce's breasts in her hands and breathing softly against the back of Joyce's neck. The sensation was tantalizing. Joyce stretched a tiny bit and Gloria stirred, her lips brushing the base of Joyce's neck. Joyce shivered and turned to face her. Gloria kissed her lips. Joyce began to speak and Gloria said "Shh..."

No need for conversation as Gloria unbuttoned Joyce's pajamas.

I t was much later than usual when Joyce walked into the lab, minus her lab coat.

Rose checked her out. "Didn't you wear those clothes yesterday?"

"Yes... need to do the wash... so busy."

Rose smiled. "Really? Gotta wash out that ice cream, huh?"

Joyce just smiled back.

* * *

O n the afternoon before the meeting at Tarth, Nash drove up to Canopy in a hybrid car with the solar panel firmly anchored to the roof. A spoiler in front of the plants broke the force of the air at high speeds. Cables ran from the roof through a hole in the hood, into the engine compartment. Everyone came out of the building and gathered around to see.

"Check this out." Nash looked serious but proud. "Any hybrid car trades off between the battery and the combustion engine, depending on conditions. This is now a *tribrid* car. The Canopy panel is light enough and generates enough juice that it makes sense to add it as a third energy source. And your panel is so efficient that when it's sunny, the panel alone can power the car. When it's parked in sunlight, energy goes into the battery. Companies have tried solar on cars before and failed. But with the Canopy, the net result is, this car uses 60% less gasoline than a hybrid car. This first take is clunky, including the meters which of course aren't integrated with the dash. I'm sure we can improve on it. But it should do for tomorrow."

"Amazing, Nash. Absolutely amazing. Gloria, can we drive this down a public freeway without jeopardizing our patent protection? Even if somebody photographs it and puts it on the internet?"

Gloria nodded. "We are good, Maxine. We already listed

powering an automobile as one application of the invention. Not that I expected it so soon."

"No one did. Nash, this will blow them away in Palo Alto. Thank you."

"My pleasure. We should probably send just one person in this car and a second car with everyone else."

"I bet you'd like to drive it."

"I bet I would."

* * *

The day of the presentation dawned clear and bright, just as Maxine had promised. A line of cars left Canopy at seven in the morning, crossed the bay and headed down to Palo Alto. Gordon met them in the Tarth parking lot. He stared at Nash's car with the contraption on top. "What's this?"

"It's a tribrid car," said Maxine. "Powered by a combustion engine, a battery, and by a Canopy roof system. Not only does it use less gas than a hybrid, it also cleans up the carbon dioxide that the engine generates even while you're driving it."

"Wow." Gordon stared at the car while Nash showed him the output on the ammeter.

Maxine continued. "And of course, the primary objective remains the same: Canopy systems on the roofs of American houses, and houses around the world."

Gordon nodded. "Let me get my partners. They all need to see this." He turned and strode into the building.

Financiers in expensive suits soon crowded around the car and mixed with the Canopy team, fielding questions at Rose, Joyce and Maxine. Most questions the founders could answer off the top. For some questions they deferred to Nash or Isis. Excitement was in the air. It was a total melee, nothing like the organized presentation the founders had carefully planned. But it was far better than anything they could have hoped for.

. . .

A t noon the Tarth staff invited the Canopy people inside for a buffet lunch, where excited conversation continued. Gordon brought his full plate over to sit with Maxine. "I can't begin to tell you how impressed we are with what we saw today. Your technology will transform the solar panel industry and has many other applications besides." He shook his head. "What a year you've had!"

"I'm glad that you and your partners see that." Maxine dotted the corner of her mouth with a linen napkin. "But Canopy research will stop if we don't get access to new quarters soon."

"Understood. Listen, we have an idea. Tarth financed a biotech company on the Richmond waterfront that unfortunately went under last month. We retained rights to the space. It's not ideal for what you want, but you might be able to make it work. Maybe five miles from your current digs in Emeryville, and about double the square footage. My partners and I want to make that available to you as part of a funding deal. And we want to do a lot more."

"Gordon, that's fantastic. When could we take possession?"

"It's empty right now. Let's make this happen. Along with a venture capital deal and coordinating with our investment bank contacts to plan a public offering." Gordon extended his hand for a handshake, but instead Maxine gave his hand a friendly squeeze. She smiled at him. "I know—we're not mixing business with pleasure. I just could not help myself."

Gordon smiled back. "Don't apologize, Max. It's all good."

T he crew from Canopy made it back to the office at four, bringing a handshake deal with Tarth Capital including new digs and a commitment of six million dollars. Maxine gathered the team in the foyer. "You were fantastic. And I don't want to jinx it, but every one of you can start thinking about what you'd like to do with the proceeds of your Canopy stock options. Now get some rest." The assembled staff applauded and, tired but happy, headed for home.

Nash parked the solar car in the loading bay behind Canopy's brick building and hugged Rose. "I'm shagged out," he said.

"You must be. Want to go by my place? I'll meet you there later."

"I won't be good for much but sleep."

"That's fine. You taking a cab?"

"Yes. And so should you. We'll sort the cars out tomorrow. See you at home, Babe."

Gloria grabbed Joyce's hand on the way out the door and said, "Why don't you come over, after you finish talking with your co-conspirators?"

Joyce grinned. "I will."

When everyone else had gone, Maxine, Rose, and Joyce sat down in the conference room, exhausted and elated. "We can actually pay ourselves now," said Maxine.

"It's about time," said Rose.

"And we can start planning our second-generation product." Joyce sat up straight to make the point.

Maxine laughed. "Joyce, we don't even have the first generation in production yet. We need to think scale-up, distribution, marketing, a thousand things we haven't dealt with yet."

"I know. And I'm not knocking what we've done so far, because it's amazing what we did in one short year. But there were lots of blind alleys. We got here by recognizing our mistakes and figuring out work arounds, one after another, because we were in such a hurry."

"Just like evolution." Rose spoke in a low voice, so tired she could barely keep her eyes open.

"Yes, I know, Rose. The power of randomness. It works but creates some clunkers, like the human appendix. At some point, and I hope it's soon, we should rethink our system from the ground up. Let's see what we can do, with the luxury of time and planning."

Maxine nodded. "Excellent point, Joyce. We absolutely can't rest on our laurels. For one thing, we already know our system doesn't work in the most extreme climates, and we need a version we can sell worldwide. And here's another thing, which I've been thinking about but haven't raised until now. Our early work upping the ante on photosynthetic algae has gotten attention from some big corporate players."

"Like who?" asked Joyce.

"The companies that supply farmers all over the world. I've been getting phone calls. I didn't want to distract you, but we need to decide what to do. These companies see the potential of our work to increase yields for many kinds of crops, and thanks to Gloria's team, we hold airtight patents on all those improvements in photosynthesis. Even the versions that didn't work for the Canopy system could have big commercial applications."

"Hey that's terrific!" Rose perked up. "Joyce's work deserves that kind of recognition."

"Indeed it does, and so does your work, Rose," said Maxine. "Right now we plan to sell our systems with plants modified to be permanently juvenile. They can't self-replicate and we control distribution. But if we were to license our underlying technology, I wonder what would happen when our hyped-up photosynthesis escaped into the natural world. We know that bioengineered crops migrate to other farmers' fields. It would only be a matter of time until they escaped into the wild. And it's obvious our plant cells would outcompete natural plants. Are we ready for a Viridian green planet Earth? And what happens to the animals that eat those plants?"

"We've let the genii out of the bottle," said Joyce.

"We've let the cat out of the bag," said Rose.

"I just hope we haven't opened Pandora's box," said Maxine. "We can refuse to license our patents if we choose. We will still make plenty of money. But patents don't last forever. Not to put a damper on this fabulous day, but it's something to ponder."

And Rose kept pondering all the way home, until she wrapped

her arms around the naked man asleep in her bed and fell asleep herself.

* * *

It was late Saturday morning and Gloria had spent the night at Joyce's house. With Gary's nod, the two women had slept in the guest room. Joyce sat between Gary and Gloria at the dining room table after breakfast. Joyce squeezed Gloria's hand and then turned to Gary. "I thought I was only attracted to testosterone-powered life forms. But then I met this woman."

Gloria was beaming. "I'm so glad you did."

Gary was trying to be a good sport, but he looked a bit shell-shocked. "I won't ask what she's got that I ain't got."

Gloria leaned over and stage-whispered to Gary, "Terrific. And I won't ask what you've got, either."

Gary looked at Gloria and then looked down at his hands, wrapped around his coffee mug, suddenly bashful. "I don't suppose you'd ever consider..."

"A threesome?" Gloria shook her head. "No. I wouldn't. I'm not ambidextrous like your wife."

Joyce nudged Gloria. "So, you're one of those rare women?"

"I am." Gloria tapped Joyce lightly on the shoulder for emphasis.

Gary gazed at the two of them and was suddenly all business. "Oh, look at the time. Gloria, great to meet you. Joyce, glad you look so happy. And I'll see you tonight?"

"Yes, you will." Joyce was still smiling and holding hands with Gloria. "Have a great day, darling."

"I'll do my best." Open minded as he believed himself to be, Gary sped out the door before his wife and her girlfriend could resume kissing.

* * *

Maxine sat across from Claudia in her Berkeley office at Dolphin Press. The publisher was beaming. "Your book is in the stores, Maxine, and the early reviews look great. Listen to this one:

'Women over fifty have long been overlooked when it comes to stories of romance, and stories of success in the executive suite. Author Maxine Vargas has done both in her new novel, *Brilliant Charming Bastard*. Female Boomers will thrill as a trio of intrepid career women outwits the treacherous Bastard and plays him at his own game. Five stars."

Maxine smiled. "Great write up. If I hadn't written the book, I'd rush right out and buy it. Thank you for everything, Claudia."

"It's been my pleasure, Maxine. A most satisfying outcome. And I can't wait to read the sequel."

"Hold on a minute, what makes you think there will be a sequel?"

"I know you, and I know your business partners. I am confident that you're bound for more adventures."

[24]

A NEW HOME

The three founders of Canopy Enterprises stood in front of a long white building on the Richmond waterfront. "It's all windows," Rose said. "We'll see the bay out the whole back of the building."

Built in the 2000s, their new headquarters looked incredibly modern. It felt enormous compared to the doomed brick building where they had gotten their start. Before they even opened the door, the three women walked all the way around the building on the encircling sidewalk. At the back were built-in lunch tables with umbrellas. Joyce peeked into a lab through the darkened glass.

"Come on, then, let's go inside and look." Maxine beckoned them to follow her around to the front door, where they entered and found a reception area. "We'll have to hire a receptionist."

"We can probably afford that, with six million in the bank." Joyce ran her fingers along the top of the reception stand.

On the far side of the lobby, inner doors led to well-lit hallways. The three women explored, their shoes clicking on the well-polished floors. There were modern labs, spacious offices, and a lunchroom where vending machines were still stocked with snacks. "These people left in a hurry," said Maxine. "I wonder what they were working on."

"They'll land on their feet somewhere," said Joyce.

The next morning, Rose and Joyce stood in one of their new labs, watching workers bring in equipment. "Didn't we just do this?" asked Rose.

Joyce laughed. "It feels that way. The past year just flew. But these labs are so—I don't know—pristine. Won't you miss the random wires hanging from the ceiling? And the ghost flushing the toilet in the middle of the night?"

Rose smiled. "And the creepy old biocontainment suits in the storage room? And the decrepit HVAC system? No, I won't. Not for one minute."

G ordon Hendricks was on the phone. "Maxine, there's someone I want you to meet. Plus I'd love to see your new headquarters. May I bring him by tomorrow?"

"Certainly, Gordon. How about ten in the morning?"

"Perfect."

"Are you going to tell me the name of your guest?"

Gordon laughed. "No, let's keep that a secret."

Maxine put on her best suit and went to work the next morning. Her new sun-filled office was the perfect place to welcome whomever Gordon had in tow.

They arrived at the white lab building that already boasted a sign saying "Canopy Enterprises" at the entrance to the well-paved lot. The bay stretched out behind the new building.

Maxine met them at the front door. Gordon introduced his guest, a stout white-haired man in a beautiful suit.

"Maxine Vargas, this is Harold Vaughn. Harold is the partner at Cummings and Stoker in charge of technology offerings."

Maxine's eyes widened. Gordon was wasting no time setting them up for a public offering. Cummings and Stoker was the top name in Silicon Valley for bringing new companies to the New York Stock Exchange. And this guy was their lead technology partner? Wow.

"So pleased to meet you, Mr. Vaughn."

"Call me Harry, please. And may I call you Maxine?"

She nodded. "Let me show you to my office. How was the drive from the Peninsula?"

"Not bad. The roads are much less crowded now that everybody's discovered working from home."

The two men settled in chairs facing Maxine's desk. As she sat down in her office chair, Maxine said, "I'm so glad you could join us in our new home. We are still moving in but I'd love to give you a tour after our meeting."

"I'd like that, Maxine." Harry opened his briefcase. "But first let's talk about how my firm can support the success of your company." He handed printed proposals to Maxine and to Gordon. "Like Tarth Capital and many others, we've been incredibly impressed by the ingenuity of your team and by your product's potential to combat global warming. I'm sure other investment banks will call on you to offer assistance with going public. But I believe we can make it happen better and faster. And I'm sure that's what you want to do, for all kinds of reasons."

"You have no idea how many reasons," said Gordon, winking at Maxine.

She managed to ignore him. "Thank you, Harry. Let's go over your proposal and I will discuss it with my business partners. One thing we will insist on is stock options for everyone who made this possible, including our interns. Each person on the Canopy team has made an essential contribution."

"Consider it done," said Harry. "Now, as to the major provisions..."

They spent a productive hour reviewing the plans from Cummings and Stoker, which were fair, detailed, and would make every person in the building rich. Or in the case of Harry and Gordon, even richer than they already were.

After a quick tour, on their way out of the building, Harry excused himself to take a phone call. While he was gone, Gordon pulled Maxine into an empty conference room and wrapped her in his arms.

"Gordon, we are still in business together."

"But not for long, Maxine. We could share a preview of things to come." His kiss was warm and soft and electrifying, and Maxine felt herself relaxing in his arms. It dawned on her that this might be the first time she had relaxed in a year.

"You're only after my money," she said, tapping his arm.

"Right. And you're only after mine," he answered.

25

LADIES AND GENTLEMEN OF THE PRESS

I t was a sunny day at the end of Spring in Richmond when Maxine, Rose and Joyce stood at a podium in front of their new labs. Over their heads, fittingly, was a green canopy decorated with the words "Canopy Enterprises." Behind them stood the rest of the team: Gloria, Nash, Marisol, Isis, Kevin and Simone. Facing them in the audience were members of the press plus the friends and family of the Canopy team. Rose waved to her daughter Linda and granddaughter Ella who were standing next to reporters. Joyce threw a kiss to her husband Gary and waved to Pam.

Maxine winked at Gordon and then turned to face her colleagues. "Alright, team, are we ready for this? I can't begin to tell you how proud I am of you all, but I'll give it a try."

In the first rank of reporters, a television journalist spoke into a camera. "We are outside the headquarters of Canopy Enterprises in Richmond, California, where company president Maxine Vargas, along with chief scientists Dr. Joyce Farrell and Dr. Rose Bingham, are about to announce progress on their solar power invention. The Canopy Roof System generates oxygen hundreds of times faster than ordinary plants. It's expected to be a game changer in slowing climate change and providing renewable energy. Ms. Vargas will be the first to speak."

Maxine stepped up to the podium. "Welcome everyone. My name is Maxine Vargas, and I am proud to serve as president and CEO of this amazing company, Canopy Enterprises. And we are thrilled to open our new headquarters here in Richmond. This day is for all of us, because it is no secret that we human beings strain the capacities of our natural world. Dr. Rose Bingham, Dr. Joyce Farrell and I started Canopy Enterprises just one year ago, with the goal of using human ingenuity to reverse the damage we humans cause to our planet. Dr. Farrell?"

J oyce cleared her throat and tapped her mike. The sound resonated across the parking lot. "To put it bluntly, nature is pissed off. She spent millions of years sequestering carbon dioxide and along came human beings and liberated it—in a hurry. Here at Canopy we improve on nature to heal nature, by changing photosynthesis in two ways: to bind more carbon dioxide, and to free more oxygen. At the same time, our system generates electrical energy without pollution. The plants we've genetically enhanced create power as well as oxygen. The covering on each panel also generates current. Our goals were ambitious, and our product, the Canopy Roof System, achieves them all."

It was Rose's turn. "Today we announce three milestones for our company, and for the planet. First, the patent for the full Canopy Roof System has been accepted for expedited review by the US Patent and Trademark Office. Altogether, half a dozen Canopy Enterprise patent applications have been accepted, thanks to the hard-working team led by our new General Counsel, Gloria Padgett. Second, our pilot plant is in validation and will produce the first commercial Canopy Roof System within three months. And third, a Public Offering of Canopy stock has been scheduled for just five months from today."

"Thank you, Dr. Bingham, Dr. Farrell." Maxine paused. "These incredible achievements were made possible by long hours and hard work on the part of the whole team: employees, consultants and interns. Ever since the pandemic, companies all over the world have been working on compressed timelines to make up for lost time. Here at Canopy, our timelines were flattened and then stomped on, and our people came through, every time. We've also had terrific support from our investors, and from Sirona Pharmaceuticals, who hosted us on their campus our first year. And so many thanks to our families and friends, who had our backs even when we doubted ourselves. Finally, we really appreciate everyone here today for helping get the word out. Thank you all."

As Maxine finished her remarks a hundred hands went up and reporters clamored to ask questions. Maxine called on a woman in the front row. "Yes?"

"Ms. Vargas, is there any connection between Canopy Enterprises and the subject of your novel, *Brilliant Charming Bastard*? Did a real-life Bastard inspire you and the other founders?

Maxine had a practiced smile ready for just this question. "Do you really think three such smart and capable women would put up with someone that annoying? Next question."

Behind Maxine, Rose whispered to Joyce, "Not much of a denial."

"Very true. But then, any denial would be a —"

"Deflection."

26

THE ROAD OF EXCESS

Six months after their press conference, Rose fidgeted in the back seat of Maxine's sedan. "When you asked us to come for a drive, I thought you meant somewhere nearby, like Tilden Park."

Maxine concentrated on steering her Maserati through the twists and turns of the Big Sur Coast Highway. "Were you one of those kids who sat in the back seat going 'Are we there yet? Are we there yet?'"

Rose laughed. "Yeah, probably."

They were driving South on a stunning California day. "It's gorgeous here." Joyce, riding shotgun, gazed out her window at the Monterey Pines and the blues and greens of the Pacific beyond.

The Mozart piece on the radio ended and a news announcer said, "Today the governor of California signed legislation requiring that beginning next year, all new roofs in the state must be biomimetic, meaning they must produce oxygen and electricity. Orders at Canopy Enterprises are expected to triple, boosting the company's stock price even higher. Other states are poised to follow California's lead and begin to undo the damage caused by fossil fuels."

The women in the car erupted in cheers.

"Yes!" Maxine turned down the radio. "We knew it was coming but it's so great to hear. Another milestone to celebrate. We're almost there, by the way."

"Almost where?" Rose tapped the back of the driver's seat.

"Here," said Maxine, easing her car into a long curving driveway on the coast side of the road.

Ahead of them, a large, Spanish-style former hotel was in the midst of renovation. Workers were everywhere, replacing clay roof tiles and replastering sections of the exterior. Other workers were visible through the windows, scraping and painting interior walls. Past the hotel, the grounds sloped down to the ocean cliffs.

Maxine stopped the car in the dilapidated parking lot. "I've brought a picnic. Will you help carry it? There's a nice view on the far side of the building." And with that, she popped the trunk and got out of the car.

They were soon settled in a patio dining area behind the old hotel. The air was balmy and a few clouds dotted the blue sky. Through a stand of live oaks was a filtered view of a rocky ocean cove.

Maxine popped a champagne bottle and invited her partners to help themselves to caprese salad and crab rolls. "Thank you both for being patient. Even you, Rose. You must have a million questions."

Joyce chose a sandwich. "I think we each do. So that's two million questions."

"I'm sure." Maxine looked thoughtful. "I've mentioned this before to Rose, but Joyce, I've always wanted to do something in honor of my mom. For decades, her salon in Oakland was an informal women's center where neighborhood ladies gathered to tell stories and share their wisdom. My project at my old law firm to encourage inventors of color was in honor of my dad, and this—" she gestured to the building behind them "—this will be to honor my mom. And I could never have done it without the two of you. That's why I'm inviting you to be founders of this new project with me."

Rose shaded her eyes. "You've done all this? You bought this place and you're renovating it?"

"Yes."

"How long have you had it?"

"My partnership buy-in was finally returned and I used it as seed money. Plus there was money from sales of the novel. And now, of course, with the great success of Canopy, there are funds to finish it."

"But what exactly will you do here?"

"It's not what *I* will do. It's what *we* will do. And not only the three of us, but women from all over the world. We'll invite women with ideas, women who want to develop inventions and policies to benefit all people. Women of wisdom, who have experienced the ups and downs of life and bring us their energy and perspective. We'll give them a safe place to try new things, and fail sometimes, and try again."

"What a grand plan," said Joyce. "Count me in."

"Me too," said Rose. "Have you chosen a name?"

"There's a line from a Blake poem that I just love," said Maxine. "'The road of excess leads to the palace of wisdom.' I'd like to call this place the Palace of Wisdom."

"The Palace of Wisdom," repeated Rose. "Fabulous. And your mom sounds terrific. I'm sure she was super proud of you. She wouldn't be surprised that you've accomplished yet another amazing thing."

Maxine gazed at her building project. "I wish she were alive to see this. Mom would love having a gathering place for women with important ideas, from all over the world."

"Maxine, this place will be fantastic." Joyce looked around, from the Palace to the sea. "It's amazing what you can do with money."

"Very true," said Rose. "And it's amazing what you can do with imagination."

"And brains," said Maxine.

"And courage," said Rose.

"And heart," said Joyce.

"Who would have thought we'd end up where we are, that first night we met at The Lab?" Maxine raised her glass. "Here's to the three of us."

"To us!" Joyce lifted her champagne.

"Yes, to us!" Rose looked at Maxine and Joyce. "The Brilliant Charming Bitches."

ABOUT THE AUTHOR

Stella Fosse

Stella Fosse is the *nom de plume* of a sixty-something retired biotechnology professional and writer who began writing sexy stories as a creative antidote to the ageism and sexism older women face in society. As a late bloomer, she writes about the pleasures and absurdities of arriving at the party just when other folks are packing up to go home.

Stella hails from California and is excited to share the joy and empowerment of writing past midlife with women in her adopted state of North Carolina. She enjoys gathering with other similarly situated women to write and laugh together.

Traditionally published works include a story in the *Dirty Old Women Anthology*, and her book *Aphrodite's Pen: The Power of*

Writing Erotica after Midlife. Stella's books are available at your local bookseller and your favorite online place. Short stories are available via all good ebook vendors as well as on her website.

She shares her writing, as well as ideas and resources for empowering women past midlife, at www.stellafosse.com. You can also find Stella Fosse on:

Facebook: facebook.com/StellaFosseAuthor
Instagram: instagram.com/stella.fosse
Twitter: twitter.com/stellafosse
LinkedIn: linkedin.com/in/StellaFosse
Goodreads: https://www.goodreads.com/StellaFosse
– please join her there.

ALSO BY STELLA FOSSE

Aphrodite's Pen: The Power of Writing Erotica After Midlife

[https://buy.bookfunnel.com/8m3bi2ibu3]

Her Poly Pod: A Love in Lockdown Story

[https://buy.bookfunnel.com/rgi7guggfr]

Dance Macabre: A Love in Lockdown Story

[https://buy.bookfunnel.com/7dm2uh2yki]

The Erotic Pandemic Ball: A Love in Lockdown Story

[https://books.stellafosse.com/pandemic]

Dirty Old Women (Anthology)

[amazon.com/dp/B01MTABT94]

Terraforming: An Erotic Nerd Tale

[https://buy.bookfunnel.com/cj1ge757xm]

* * *

FREE TEN DAY CLASS: WRITE YOUR EROTIC JOURNEY THROUGH THE DECADES OF LIFE

[https://page.stellafosse.com/journey]

CREATE A SEXY STORY WITH STELLA A FREE SEVEN DAY WRITING COURSE

[https://page.stellafosse.com/news_write]

PLEASE REVIEW THIS BOOK!

A Review is one of the biggest favors you can do for an author —
especially on the larger vendors' sites.

Reviews are the lifeblood of writers because they let other readers
— and potential readers — know what you thought of their work.
Some topics to consider:

What struck you about this book?

What did you think of the storylines?

What was your opinion of the writing?

How about the editing?

What do you want to say about this book to other readers?

Please write an honest review on whichever web platform you prefer.
Stella is on all the major platforms and you all know your favorite!

Stella is also on Goodreads.

BOOK CLUB DISCUSSION QUESTIONS

1. In the Spring of 2021, three young women discovered on Instagram that they were dating the same Boise college student. They became friends, broke up with the young man, and spent the summer touring in an old bus they renovated together. Articles about them appeared in the *Washington Post* and elsewhere. How surprising is it for women in that situation to become friends and collaborators, as did Rose, Joyce and Maxine in the novel?

2. The average romance reader is a woman in her fifties and many romance writers are women past midlife, but publishers often encourage them to write characters in their twenties. Some publishers categorize books about women in their ***thirties*** as "seasoned," or senior, romance. How does writing and reading about older characters push back on sexism and ageism?

3. Investors in Silicon Valley often ask female entrepreneurs about Elizabeth Holmes, the disgraced founder of a California biotechnology company whose trial on criminal fraud charges began in August 2021. One industry columnist even wrote an article

comparing the female founder of a legitimate biotech company to the infamous Holmes and her company, Theranos. How does this blatant sexism compare with the funding issues faced by Rose, Joyce and Maxine in the novel?

4. As women in their sixties, Maxine, Joyce and Rose explore their sexuality in various ways. How do their experiences resonate (or not) for you? Which of the romantic plotlines in the book most interested you and why?

5. The setting of the book, the San Francisco Bay Area, is mentioned frequently in the novel. How engaging did you find that setting?

6. At what point in the story were you most interested? Did the novel end as you expected?

7. What would you say are the main themes of the book? Has the author explored them in ways that interest you?

To arrange a video discussion with Stella Fosse for your book club, please write to Stella's publicist at graham@stellafosse.com.

And please follow Stella's blogs and newsletters at www. stellafosse.com.

ACKNOWLEDGMENTS

If it takes a village to raise a novel, *Brilliant Charming Bastard* is a shining example.

This book is about the power of women together, and it came about because of women who stood united. When Lynx Canon began the "Dirty Old Women" reading series in Oakland, California, she called together a sisterhood that inspires one another to this day. An outgrowth of that reading series, the Elderotica writing group, provided fun and structured play space for women who were new to writing and experienced at life. And that in-person group led directly to online Elderotica groups during the pandemic that included women on several continents. Many thanks to these sisters, and to novelists like Rae Padilla Francoeur, Pamela Skjolsvik and Sally Bellerose, who write superbly about the vivid sexy lives of women after midlife. Each story we publish builds a strong new narrative about the power of older women.

I also can't thank Diana Rosinus enough for bringing the novel to life with her marvelous cover design. And my editor and publisher, Graham Bird, provided patient and tireless support to this effort from day one to publication. Thanks also to Judith Stanton for her detailed proofreading. Any remaining errors are my own.

And finally, thank you, dear Reader, for witnessing the adventures of Rose, Joyce and Maxine through the East Bay biotech scene. May you find inspiration to write sexy tales grounded in your own vivid life.

CPSIA information can be obtained
at www.ICGtesting.com
Printed in the USA
FSHW010508081121
86045FS